How to Write Fiction

Tools and Techniques

E.E. "Doc" Murdock

Includes three original stories
"built" step by step

H.O.T. Press

Published by

H.O.T. Press
Los Angeles

www.hotpresspublishing.com

Publishing fine books since 1983

ISBN: 0-923178-27-9
ISBN-13: 978-0-923178-27-7

Acknowledgments

I am indebted to the members of the Ojai Writing Workshop who provided valuable feedback as I worked through the many drafts of this book. I would also like to acknowledge the help of all my students at California State University, Long Beach who taught me so much.

Most importantly, I want to acknowledge my co-teacher and life partner Zoe Murdock who contributed a great deal of wisdom and insight to this book. Without her, this book would not exist.

Novels by E.E. "Doc" Murdock

- **The Pain Artist: An American *Hikikomori***

- **My Vietnam War**

- **A Psalm for Cock Robin**: A Harp and His (Dead) Mother Mystery

- **Crueltown**: A Drew Steele Los Angeles-Las Vegas Mystery

- **The End of the Civil War**: A Drew Steele Civil War Mystery

- **Who Owns Arizona**: A Drew Steele Civil War Mystery

Table of Contents

1

Introduction

The first stories were undoubtedly verbal tales of adventure, about hunting and exploring, about battles and conquests. And who could blame those first storytellers if they spiced up their stories a bit with fictional descriptions of unexpected perils and near disasters they overcame. Such fictional "additions" could be seen as the first storytelling techniques. They were designed to get the storyteller's audience more interested in the story.

Storytelling *technique* has been constantly evolving since then, but the goal is still the same—get your readers interested in the story right from the first sentence and keep them interested all the way through to the last word.

That's what this book is about. It shows you, step by step, how to use modern storytelling tools and techniques that will get your readers interested in your stories. In this book, I describe a unique set of interest-creating tools and techniques a fiction writer can add to his or her writing toolbox, and then I show how these techniques can be used to create a complete story.

To make the story creation process *concrete* instead of abstract, I will "build" three original example stories that demonstrate three different narrative approaches to storytelling—first-person, second-person, and third-person. I plan to create these example stories in a way that illustrates as many different fiction writing tools and tech-niques as possible, and I'll discuss my fiction-writing *thought pro-cesses* in each stage of the story creation process.

Along the way, I'll also provide a lot of fiction-writing "tips" that will look like this:

TIP:
Watch for writing tips and suggestions in these special "tip" sections. They provide information about useful writing techniques you can use in your own stories.

The Tools of Creative Writing

It's best to think about learning to write fiction as a *process* that's similar to the process of learning how to create a beautiful oil painting. Before you can begin to create your painted masterpiece, you have to learn to use the required tools. You have to learn about all the different kinds of brushes and how to use them properly. You have to learn about the different kinds of paints and surfaces. You have to learn about light and shadow, about color and shading and texture. Then comes the long periods of practice that can lead to skill development and the evolution of a personal style. Once the basic tools and techniques of oil painting have been mastered, students often go to museums to study the techniques of the masters.

You should think about fiction writing much in the same way: first, you have to learn about the tools and techniques of creative writing, and then you have to practice using them. It is also important to study how skilled writers apply those techniques. Only then will you be ready to undertake masterful creative writing. It's not easy, but once you learn the techniques, it is *very* rewarding.

Getting Feedback

You should actively **solicit feedback** on your stories, and not just from your friends and family (they will always tell you it's great). One of the best ways to get useful feedback on your writing is to sign up for a **writing workshop** (not a writer's *group*) at a university or perhaps at a public library. There is no better way to objectively "see" your own writing than to get feedback on it from a good teacher and from other skilled writers. That said, *subjective* feedback like "It didn't grab me," or "I don't think the character would do that" isn't going to help you much. But *objective,* reader-oriented criticism like "I think you need to spend more words on conveying how the protagonist felt about being rejected," or "I don't think you've developed the character's backstory enough for the reader to believe your protagonist would do that" *is* very helpful because it focuses on a writing issue and suggest how to improve it.

Be aware that not all feedback—even if it comes in a writing workshop—is going to be useful feedback. Every human sees a story in their own unique way, so you have to learn how to judge the value of the feedback you get. But you should never ignore any feedback; instead, try to think through which techniques you were using that made readers react to your story the way they did.

One more thing about writing workshops: always thank every person that gives you feedback, even if you didn't think the feedback was useful. If you act like you didn't value a person's feedback, that person *and* the other members of the workshop will be less likely to give you much feedback in the future. All feedback is valuable, even if it is only *reader feedback* (how a reader reacted to your story).

Be aware that the most useful feedback is often the most *critical* feedback. One of the hardest things for writers to see is the flaws in their own writing. Although it may hurt to find out your writing isn't as perfect as you thought it was, critical feedback from fellow writers shows they are serious about your writing and are trying to help you.

In addition to getting valuable feedback on *your* stories, you can learn a surprising amount about writing in a workshop by learning how to critique the stories of other writers. Also, it's a lot easier to see the kinds of mistakes you are making when you see them show up in the writing of others.

The Example Stories

First-person. I will create a first-person story in which a character is both *in* the story and the one narrating the story. A first-person storyteller is *usually* the central character in the story (the *protagonist*), referring to himself or herself using *first-person pronouns* such as *I* or *me*. However, first-person storytellers can also be *peripheral* to the story, in the role of observer.

Second Person. I will create a story that uses second-person pronouns. Although some books on creative writing list three points of view, first, second, and third, there is actually no such thing as a second-person *point of view*. (How can the use of the second-person pronoun "you" be considered a point of view? Whose story is it? Yours?) Nevertheless, using *second-person pronouns* in a story can create an interesting effect, as we will see in Chapter 3.

Third-person. I will create a third-person story that uses an unknown and unknowable narrator that serves as an *intermediary* between the story events and the reader. The story will still have a main character, a protagonist, but that character is not the storyteller. This type of narrator refers to the characters in the story by name or by using *third-person pronouns* such as he or she.

2

Writing the First-Person Story

A first-person story is one in which a character *in the story* appears to be telling the story. That *first-person narrator* refers to himself or herself using first-person pronouns such as "I" or "me." (It's also possible for stories to be told in plural first-person using pronouns like "we" and "us," but that's fairly unusual.)

Most writers begin their fiction writing careers by writing a personal story. That's not a good idea. Why? Because writing a personal story is handcuffing yourself. If you want to be a *fiction* writer, why limit yourself to writing about real places and real events? The joy of writing fiction lies in making up characters and places and situations and events. Story events need to happen when it's time for them to happen in order to systematically move the story forward. Characters in stories need to do what they need to do in order to *get the reader vicariously involved* (one of the main goals of storytelling). As the writer of the story, it's your job not only to create the fictional story events, but also to give the fictional characters fictional personalities and motivations that make fictional sense.

In first-person stories, the storyteller has to play two roles, the *narrator role* (telling the reader what is happening in the *world of the story*) and the *character role* (conveying the protagonist's reactions to story events).

TIP:

To create a story, a writer has to create a **diegetic universe**, a world that only exists within the story. A fiction writer must create **the world of the story** by conveying clear images of story events, clear descriptions of places that exist within the story, and well-drawn characters that occupy that world. It is the writer's responsibility to clearly convey the world of the story to the reader.

Typical uses of the narrative role are to describe story action (both cars ran the red light) and to move time forward (the next day). Using the character role, the story is told *through* the perceptions of the protagonist, which provides a unique "take" on the story events. In the narrative role, information is presented to the reader as a set of facts. Unfortunately, that leaves the protagonist out of the interaction. Instead of using narrative writing like "Sally walked into the room," you could convey the same information with "Here comes Sally, walking right in like she owns the place." See the difference? The first method of describing Sally's entrance into the room could be told by anybody. It is a disembodied storytelling narrator that flatly describes story action to the reader, leaving the protagonist completely out of the story. The second version also describes the action, *and* at the same time, provides the reader with information about the protagonist's view of it.

Sometimes writers even use the narrative role to *tell* the reader what is going on *inside* the protagonist by writing "I was really angry," versus *showing* how the protagonist feels with "That was the final straw, but I tried not to let my anger show." The *showing* version is much more likely to engage the reader. Finding ways to *show* story events through the protagonist's personal perceptions gets the reader more vicariously involved in the story, and that is key to creating a story that the reader will find compelling. One of the main advantages of writing a story in first-person is that you can characterize a protagonist through *the way* he or she tells the story. Everything first-person protagonists do, say, or think *characterizes them.*

Getting the Story Started

One of the most common questions student writers ask is, *How do you start a new story?* Many writers will try to "think up" a complete story before they start writing. That is very hard to do. In fact, it's the main cause of *writer's block.*

The best solution to writer's block is to avoid the advance planning stage altogether. Don't sit there thinking about what your story is going to be *about*; instead, think about *an interesting character.*

All stories involve **characters**, even if those characters are puppies or goldfish or brave little ants. Therefore, it is always best to start the story-creation process by creating a character.

TIP:

If the story is mostly focused on a protagonist's *personal* challenge or a personal goal or dilemma of some kind, it is known as a **character-driven** story. The story will be *about* the character as he or she tries to achieve something or tries to find a solution to a personal problem.

Once you "get to know" your character, you can start writing about what that character would do in a specific situation.

If you can create an interesting character and then put that character into an interesting situation—some kind of problem that needs to be solved by the end of the story—you will end up with a good *character-driven story*.

I call that approach "walking the character." If you really understand your character, once you put that character into a situation, the character will "tell you" what he or she needs to do and say.

If you try to outline your entire story, you trap yourself into story events and plot issues that may not work once the story is actually underway. As you "get to know" your protagonist and begin to understand his or her motives and personality, the story will evolve based on the protagonist's goals.

However, you still need to come up with the opening sentences. But don't let yourself get stuck there: you don't have to create the "perfect" first sentence, just get something to get the story started. You will probably change the opening later anyhow during the revision process.

So, if you decide to begin your first-person story by thinking of a character, how do you "find" that character? You don't want to handicap yourself by writing about real people in your real town, but it's not a bad idea to write about *the kinds* of people you know and put them into *situations you understand.*

To start a story, you need to make up a character you can "get inside of" and write convincingly about. I often write a lot of notes about my imagined protagonist before I actually begin the story.

TIP:

Notice that even though I haven't created any characters yet, I'm already *referring to my protagonist as "him."* Although it's interesting to imagine creating a protagonist not of your gender, it can lead to problems. Your readers are going to be seeing the world of the story through the perceptions of your protagonist, so you want to be sure you fully understand his or her motivations and sensibilities.

While the story events that occur in a character-driven story should be interesting, they *should not* be the main reason readers keep on reading. In a character-driven story, readers will be interested in how the character is going to deal with his situation. I call that the story's *vicariousness.*

If a story has *a high degree of vicariousness*, readers will be much more likely to get fully involved while reading it.

Once you have created your protagonist and put that character into some kind of situation that challenges him, you should keep an open mind about where the story is heading. You will be much more likely to create a good *character-driven* story that will engage your readers if you let the story go where it wants to go. In other words, think character, not *plot.*

The next step in getting your story started is to create the first of a sequence of *story events,* presented to the reader as *scenes.* The sequence of scenes systematically *lead* the reader to a conclusion by the end of the story. (The concept of the *arrow of plot* implies a relentless drive forward.)

That idea that you should constantly be *leading* (or enticing) the reader forward is something you will see throughout this book. You should always be thinking about your story in terms of what the reader is getting out of it. That means you, the writer, should always be thinking about where you are leading the reader.

Sometimes that actually gets down to the sentence-by-sentence level: you should not only be thinking about where each scene is leading the reader, you should also make sure there are no "wasted" sentences. Each sentence should, in some way, lead the reader forward.

As the reader accumulates information from the story events, they should *feel* the story relentlessly driving toward a known (or implied) end.

TIP:

Plot is one of the most important concepts in creative writing, but many might find it hard to formally state what the plot of their story is. It's best to think of plot in reader terms: it's what keeps the reader reading, what keeps the reader interested. That means, you should introduce the plot at the beginning of your story and keep it going from start to end. Think of plot as a golden thread that weaves its way through the story events that make up the tapestry of your story. Sometimes writers get so involved in weaving in story events, they forget to keep weaving in that golden thread of plot.

Okay, let's start mapping out an example first-person story. Let's begin by thinking about what type of protagonist we should create, while still holding back any thoughts about what kind of story we're going to write.

Because my first PhD was in child psychology, I often like to write about young protagonists who are in the process of learning about life.

So, lets start our example story with that concept in mind. Let's say we're going to write a story about a young person who is dealing with a challenging life lesson.

Such stories are known as *coming-of-age* stories. In fact, every story about a young protagonist has the potential to be a coming-of-age story because it is quite likely that a teen or pre-teen protagonist will still be learning major life lessons. In such stories, how the protagonist deals with those life lessons becomes *the plot*.

Now, how old should our protagonist be? It's important to decide on the age of the protagonist right at the beginning because the kinds of values a person has will often be determined by their age. Character-driven stories are all about hopes and fears, and our hopes and fears change as we grow older. For now, let's just say he is a teenager, about fifteen or so. Many stories have been written about that period of life because it is so formative.

However, when writing about a young protagonists, you have to be aware of first-person *unreliability*.

TIP:

Unlike stories told from the point of view (POV) of an authoritarian **third-person narrator** who is not "in" the story, readers may not always believe a first-person narrator to be a *reliable* source of information.

The term "**unreliable narrator**" itself is interesting because it is defined in terms of what you, the writer, expects the reader to believe or not believe. Portraying protagonist **unreliability** is an interesting technique when done intentionally, but it can be troublesome if the reader does not believe your protagonist when he or she makes a statement of belief that you want the reader to accept.

As the phenomenological philosophers say, reality is a first-person experience (we all see the world in our own unique way), and that means you have to work extra hard in first-person to be absolutely sure the reader is "getting" the meaning your protagonist intended.

That is especially true when the protagonist is young or mentally challenged. That kind of protagonist will often be seen as unreliable because he or she may not *know* what is true and what is not.

Our first task will be to create a *believable* young protagonist who is dealing with a formative life experience. We will have to get the reader interested in how he's going to deal with that life experience.

Next, we have to think about the *locale* in which our story will take place. For this first demonstration story, to show how place shapes character, let's say he's still living in the place he grew up in.

The locale will, to some degree, determine how the characters in the story talk and act.

I grew up in the Midwest, so following my own advice about writing what you know about, let's say our young protagonist grew up in the Midwest, and he is still there.

Our story is beginning to take shape. Now that we have a young protagonist from the Midwest, let's add a bit more detail about the setting.

Let's say he grew up in a rural environment, say somewhere that's far away from the big cities that surround the Great Lakes. And to give the place more character, let's say it's a small town.

Small towns have "character" because their populations are more homogeneous than in cities. There are often a few local "characters" that everybody knows.

We now have a young protagonist who is still living in the small town he grew up in. In fact, I think we should imagine him as never having ventured very far from that small town.

Now it's time to start thinking how to get the story going. We still don't need to think about the plot.

Character-driven stories are about what a character wants, so once we figure out what our character *wants*, the plot will be obvious.

As I said earlier, I'm going to try to incorporate as many different storytelling elements as possible in these example stories. So, to demonstrate how to handle dialect, let's have our young protagonist think and speak in a way that is characteristic of a region.

When writing dialect, it's *not necessary* to make every utterance sound regional; often you can represent regional speech with simple techniques like dropping the "g" from the ends of some words (like walkin or thinkin).

You can also use parts of words, like cept (instead of except). You can also use region-specific word replacements like ya (instead of you) or yep (instead of yes).

It may take some research, but you can often find examples of region-specific phrases, like "he done wrong" or "spect we hafta get er done."

However, be careful not to overdo that kind of thing in a serious story lest you make your story seem comedic.

Back in the day, writers like Mark Twain made sure nearly every sentence of dialogue contained unusual pronunciations and phrasing. They tried to capture *all* of a character's speech patterns. However, it is now more common to just *indicate* a character's regional or cultural dialect.

TIP:

Be aware that there is a difference between the way a protagonist speaks and the literary concept of first-person "**voice**." That concept of voice in first-person fiction writing does not refer to dialogue; it refers to how the storyteller tells the story, his attitudes, opinions, and personal "take" on things. "Voice" characterizes the storyteller. If your storyteller has a recognizable storytelling voice, it will get the reader more interested in that character, which is one of the main goals in a character-driven story.

Next, let's narrow down the locale even more. Let's make our protagonist a resident of the southern Mississippi river valley, say somewhere in southwestern Illinois.

In fact, let's put him in a small town that's close by that big river and make our story have something to do with the Mississippi River itself. It's one of the longest rivers on the planet, and it will undoubtedly be well known to just about every reader, even if they've never seen it in person.

There have been so many great stories written about the Mississippi River, the river itself has almost become a literary figure. Mark Twain's adventure stories of Tom Sawyer and Huck Finn take place on the Mississippi River, and the nature of the river and the people of that region play an important role in those stories. And in Faulkner's short novel, *Old Man,* the story is about the people of that region, and the Mississippi River *is* the old man of the book's title.

We have a general idea of our protagonist (a young man who grew up in a small town near the Mississippi River) we can start to think about what kind of personal crisis he would run into.

That reminds me of something I saw when I was a child in Illinois. On a visit to the Mississippi River with my parents, I saw the local authorities in a boat "dragging" the river. They were looking for the body of a missing person. Going back to the idea that we should write about something you know about, I think I'll make that the main focus of the story: the authorities are dragging the river for a body.

Now that we have a protagonist, a locale, and a focus for the story, the beginning of the story practically writes itself. Somebody important to the protagonist is missing and the authorities are dragging the

river for the body. Let's make the missing person the protagonist's little sister. That sets up a character-driven plot: how would a young
man deal with such a crisis?

Let's start the story by having our young protagonist think about
what has happened. We can use his thoughts to inform the reader of
the season, the state of the river, and the environment in which the
story is going to take place.

> **If my little sister woulda gone under the mighty
> Mississippi River durin the fall, or even when the win-
> ter is just startin to come on and the patches of thin
> silvery ice get to spreadin across the backwater shal-
> lows, they mighta been able to see her body down
> there on the bottom just by lookin down into the water
> usin their bottom-looker, that tube they got with the
> glass in the end of it.**
>
> **But in the late springtime, like it is now, the big ol
> Missip is near in flood stage and the water gets so
> muddy you can't even see your hand when you stick it
> in up to the elbow. When the river gets that muddy,
> they hafta drag for the bodies.**

These two opening paragraphs provide the reader with story information by having our protagonist think about what has happened. By
starting right out in the protagonist's point of view, it informs the
reader about the situation, but perhaps more importantly, it informs
the reader that the story is going to be told through protagonist perception.

The way our protagonist thinks about what has happened shows
his approach to dealing with the situation. He may be young and
unsophisticated, but the way he tells the story shows he thinks deeply
about things. He is somewhat analytical, and he is fairly calm, despite
the dire situation.

The protagonist's "take" on the situation informs the reader of
some important story facts. He thinks his little sister has "gone under"
the river, and the time of year is late spring. He also assumes "they"
are going to drag the river to try to find her body.

The beginning *contains* (as in *limits*) the story. The reader knows
the story is going to be "seen" from the point of view of a protagonist,
and it is going to be focused on one significant event.

Writers sometimes "beat about the bush" before they get the *real* story going. They try to put in too much information about the setting and the environment instead of dropping the reader right into the "real" story. We will eventually have to provide the reader with more information about the setting, but there will be plenty of time to do that once we have established the protagonist and the situation.

TIP:

Notice that I've decided to tell this story in present **tense**. Most first-person stories are told in *past tense* simply because that makes logical sense: the story has already happened, so the way of describing it should be in the past tense. However, many modern stores are being told in *present tense*—even first-person stories. Although it can be more of a challenge to work with, present tense creates more of a sense of immediacy, as if the outcome is not already known.

I've decided to start this story with the sister already missing and presumed drowned. I could have started at some earlier point, say by creating a scene in which the boy first learns about what happened to his sister. I could have even started earlier by creating a scene that shows the reader what the boy's day-to-day life is like. But as I said, it's important to *contain* your story by restricting it to whatever is going to be the main focus. In this case, I want the focus of the story to be on the dragging of the river and the protagonist's response to it.

TIP:

When writing a first-person character-driven story, it works well to create a protagonist who is **good observer** and a **good reporter**. However, it should not feel like your protagonist is talking *to* the reader. You should try to make his reporting more like he is *thinking* about the situation, going over it in his mind.

I began the story by having our young protagonist think through what he has just heard, that his little sister is missing and is reported to have drowned herself in the river. He should continue to think about the situation in a way that characterizes him. His response to the situation should give us the beginnings of the kind of character-driven story that will draw the reader in.

TIP:

I call a protagonist's reaction to story events the **two-step.** The two steps are (1) the story event, and (2) the protagonist's response to that event. The protagonist's response can be in the form of **action, dialogue,** or **thought,** but in order to keep the reader vicariously involved, he should respond to pretty much ever story event.

The **two-step** is one of the most useful techniques used in modern character-driven fiction, so much so that many modern stories and novels are *all about* how the protagonist responds to story events. If you make your protagonist a good observer and have him share his reactions to what he observes, you can tell the story "through" his perceptions. It's a way to **show** story events unfolding rather than **telling** the story to the reader using the narrative role.

By having our protagonist drop the Gs off of words that should end in "ing" and by having him use words like "woulda" (in place of "would have"), we are giving him a somewhat rural, somewhat southern sounding "voice."

By the way, I am not using the customary apostrophes to replace missing letters because I'm trying to represent regional speech as if words like durin and startin were part of the normal vernacular for these characters. The use of a lot of apostrophes might feel (to the reader) unnatural and too formal for these types of characters.

Okay, we have a situation and a rural-sounding protagonist through which readers are being given access to the world of the story. Now, we can give the reader a bit of information about what happened earlier in the day. Again, we need to make sure the information is given to the reader in a way that makes it seems like it's coming from protagonist rather than the author.

> **This mornin, when the sheriff and his deputy were gettin ready to start draggin the river, I saw em tyin some long wires to the back end of their old wood boat. Then they tied some big ol sharp and real mean-lookin treble-hooks onto the ends of them wires.**

The description, "Big ol sharp and real mean-lookin," conveys story information to the reader, and at the same time, gives some idea of our protagonist's "take" on what he saw.

So far, our protagonist has been mostly giving the reader information about *the situation* (a drowning and an ensuing search for the body) and *the setting* (the river). Assuming the reader is now "into" the story, let's have our protagonist watch the dragging of the river and think about what he is seeing.

> **Now, as I'm sittin here on the riverbank watchin em go back and forth, first upstream and then back down again, with the sheriff standin up at the back of the boat keepin the drag lines from gettin all tangled up, I try not to think about those sharp hooks too much. I don't want to even imagine what those sharp things would do to her soft little body if they do snag her up.**

This paragraph is a good example of *the two-step method* I described earlier. The story event he's observing (the dragging of the river) is *step one,* and his response to it (his imagining of what those terrible hooks would do to his little sister's body), is *step two.*

These opening paragraphs say a lot about who the protagonist is, and it is done without *telling* the reader about him; he is *characterized* by the way he looks at things rather than what he looks like. Although many short stories begin by describing the protagonist physically, let's see if we can find a way to do that later without using the narrator role.

Next, let's have the protagonist provide the reader with more information about the most important off-stage character in this story, the missing sister. We can do it with a follow-on thought about what the terrible dragging hooks would do to his little sister's soft body.

> **Even though she was only a year younger than me, she was a little thing. Not tall and gangly like me. Ma always says the two of us are so different it's hard to believe we both came out of her. But we do both got the same blonde hair, even though mine is getting darker as I get older. Unlike me, she had a sort of softness to her, ever since she was little. Softness in her bein too.**

Using protagonist thought, I've provided the reader with information about the sister, and by comparing her to himself, the reader now has more information about what our protagonist looks like. Readers usually like to have a least a general idea of what a protagonist looks like, but a first-person narrator has no easy way to describe himself. Having your protagonist compare himself to other characters in the story is a good way to provide that kind of information.

Many writers feel the need to describe the protagonist early in the story. But in a character-driven story, only basic physical descriptions are necessary. There is little need to employ *the old mirror trick*, having the first-person storyteller describe seeing himself in a mirror. In fact, that method of self-description has been used so often, it's become something of a cliché.

Some writers might try to get a description of the protagonist into the story by switching into the point of view of another character. That approach abruptly changes the reader's perception of *who* the story is about. You might very well lose the reader's vicarious involvement with the protagonist that you worked so hard to establish. Although there are no absolute "rules" in fiction, there are some very useful guidelines, and the guideline about *sticking to one point of view,* unless you have *a good reason* to change, is an important one.

If something about a protagonist's physical appearance is important to the story, it can be gradually filtered in at some point by showing how his physicality affects him (with my bum leg, I can't get there very fast) or by having other characters in the story refer to it in dialogue ("sorry to hear about your broke leg").

That said, there are some types of stories in which it *is* appropriate to switch the point of view. For example, romance stories sometimes switch back and forth between two main characters, often in alternate chapters. The "romance technique" tips off the reader that the two characters are going to get together later in the story.

Another example where there might be more than one point of view character, are stories in which there is a protagonist and an antagonist (if they are of relatively equal importance).

There are also stories in which the point of view of characters who are observing the protagonist is important to the plot. I'll try to create a story like that when I start building my example third-person story.

TIP:
Some of the protagonist's thoughts about his sister are conveyed to the reader using the **sentence fragments** (Softness in her bein too). Sentence fragments can help make it "feel" more like character thought.

The protagonist's description of his sister using the phrase "softness in her bein" is a hint to the reader about what might have happened to her.

Writers should keep in mind the fact that readers are aware (at least subconsciously) that all information the author puts into a story is there for a reason. They may not stop to think, "I wonder why the author inserted that phrase "softness in her bein" into the story, but at some level, they will probably be aware that these *plot hints* are somehow important to the complex fabric of the evolving story.

The passage describes the sister through the perceptions of the protagonist. He is thinking about her in the past tense, as if he's decided she really has drowned. Again, readers may or may not notice his use of past tense, but at some level, they may start out assuming—along with the protagonist—that she is dead.

Some writers might feel like they have to describe a character like the sister in greater detail. For example, a writer might be tempted to squeeze in a description such as "Those hooks would really hurt my little sister who has light brown hair and brown eyes and is only five foot two and weighs less than one hundred pounds." Useful information perhaps, but why would the protagonist be having such a thought? He knows what his sister looks like. And what would her hair and eye color and her height have to do with the softness of her body? If such information is important to the story, it can be filtered in later, maybe by having the authorities ask him to describe her.

TIP:

Writers are sometimes unable to resist the temptation to fully describe characters and scenes when such descriptions are not all that important to the plot. If you put in *too much* information, you can **dilute** the story. If you interrupt the flow of the story by putting in irrelevant information, it lessens the importance of the information that actually furthers the plot.

Next, we need to provide the reader with some *backstory* (events that occurred before the time frame of the story) about why he thinks his sister is in the river.

> **Maybe that's why ma thinks she probly went and threw herself in the river.**

This one line reveals to the reader that "the fact" that the sister has drowned in the river may or may not actually be true. I haven't created any actual eyewitnesses to the supposed drowning; therefore, it is only the mother's *feeling* that her daughter "probably" threw herself in the river. The girl's mother apparently is so sure her daughter has thrown herself in the river and drowned, the sheriff has begun dragging the river to look for her. For the reader, this brings a new plot issue into the story: is the boy's little sister actually in the river? Is this a suicide story, or a delusional-mother story?

And because this is a character-driven story that focuses on the mother's son, the reader will want to know what he thinks about his mother's "feeling." Is it his "duty" to believe what his mother believes, or does he have doubts about it? That issue now becomes another aspect of the plot.

Will the reader therefore trust the mother's opinion and the son's willingness to go along with it, or will they now have doubts about it? So far, our protagonist hasn't voiced any doubts about the drowning story.

At the start of the story, the sheriff began dragging the river to try to find the little girl's body. But does that necessarily mean the sheriff believes in the mother's opinion? Let's insert a little more backstory about that using protagonist memory.

> **The sheriff told ma that maybe we oughta hold off on the draggin for a bit cause the girl'd only been gone the one day. But ma told him she'd got a hard feelin that her little girl is down under that muddy ol water.**

Here, we have a backstory moment in which our protagonist summarizes, through memory, a conversation between the mother and the sheriff that indicated the sheriff had doubts about the mother's "hard feeling," but agreed to start the dragging process anyhow.

This passage builds on *the unreliability issue.* Managing protagonist unreliability can be tricky because readers generally believe what protagonists believe. Therefore, you have to find a way to tip off the reader that the beliefs of the protagonist may not be accurate.

Now, let's bring the reader's attention back to our protagonist and show the reader where he is and what he is thinking.

> **What with ma thinkin Sis is out there drowned in the river, I didn't go to school today. I just been sittin here on the riverbank all mornin watchin the draggin.**

This passage clearly places the protagonist in the role of observer and reporter of story action. In that role, we should now have him describe, in some detail, what the dragging process looks like.

The dragging of a river to look for a body is not something many readers will have seen. Therefore, it is worth spending a fair number of words on what the process looks like—from the point of view of the protagonist of course. It should be done in a way that "feels" like that particular person would see it.

> **The sheriff's old boat takes on water some, and the boat motor is pretty weak, so they don't hardly make any progress goin upstream against the current. But once they get a ways upstream, they get their boat turned around and shut off the motor so they can just float downstream until they get to the sandbar that's all the way down almost to Linden's bend. I guess they figure if she didn't get caught on the river bottom or hung up on that sandbar, she'll be long gone down the**

> **river to who knows where.**
>
> **Every time they get their boat floated down to the sandbar, the deputy has to pull the motor's starter cord a bunch of times, cussin and cussin, til he finally gets it goin again, and then they come putt-puttin their way back up here again.**

In addition to providing the reader with information about the river dragging process, the passage also brings the reader's attention to a new character in the story, the deputy. Hopefully, because the deputy is only *helping* the sheriff, and because I limit my description of him to his task, I will have successfully tipped the reader off to the fact that he *is not* going to play a significant role in the story.

TIP:

Supporting-cast characters (characters other than the star of the show, the protagonist) can be of many different types. Some are mere **walk-ons**, like a waiter or a bartender. You should not name such characters, give them lines of dialogue, or physically describe them in any detail. To do so would indicate to the reader that they *are not* mere walk-ons and that they will, sooner or later, play an important role in the story. On the other hand, if a supporting-cast character *is* going to play an important role later in the story, you can foreshadow that fact by giving him or her a name and by providing the reader with a terse (but memorable) description.

If I wanted the reader to pay attention to the deputy, I could have described him as one of those long and lanky guys who is a lot stronger than he looks, a heavy drinker who is well known to the regulars at the local bar but who always somehow manages to get his act together and quickly sober up when it's time to resume his part-time deputy job. (But that's not the character I'm creating in this story, so erase that description from your mind.)

Even though the protagonist often focuses on the sheriff, he too shall go unnamed. The sheriff is a special type of supporting-cast character, one who plays an important role in the story, but it is a role that is important not because of *who he is* as an individual, but only because *he is* the sheriff. His role in the story is to do what sheriffs do.

Now, while we have a lull in the story as our protagonist watches them drag the river, let's do a little more characterizing of him.

Obviously, he should be thinking about what's going on, but having him just sit there doing nothing as he watches the dragging would be boring to the reader.

Why don't we have him do something active to help characterize him *and* the place.

> **While I watch em go draggin back and forth, I pass the time by throwin punched-out clam shells at the water. Them punched-out clam shells are layin all over the place. Piles of em, left over from the old pearl button factory that's been closed since even before I was born. Don't know why the factory closed down. No clams left in this ol river, I guess. Some say all them clams got done in by oil that leaks out of the oil barges that pass by here day and night. Maybe so, maybe not. It could just be that the button factory caught so many clams there weren't none left.**

Creating the scene of our protagonist throwing shells into the water not only helps set the scene in the reader's mind, the fact that the place is littered with punched-out clam shells suggests the town *used* to be a place of industry. Now the discarded clam shells are only remnants of a bygone day. The left-over, punched-out clam shells convey old and worn out. In addition, our protagonist's thoughts about why the factory closed down also suggest industrial pollution.

Now let's bring action, and even sound, into the scene.

> **I stand up and toss them punched-out shells out into the river as far as I can. If I throw 'em hard enough, the holes in those shells make a whistlin sound as they fly out over the water. It's kind of a lonesome sound, and it makes me think of how Sis always liked to hum songs to herself while she was out all alone in**

> the garden doin her hoein. I get kind of sad remem-
> berin her when she was hummin like that. I think
> maybe her hummin like that meant she was at least a
> little bit happy, which she wasn't very often.
>
> Another reason I throw em so hard is cause I'm
> feelin kinda mad. If she really is out there drowned,
> and they drag her body up, I'm gonna get even mad-
> der cause maybe I coulda done somethin to prevent it.
> Maybe I coulda played with her more, or at least
> talked to her more. I don't know why I didn't. Cause
> she was a girl I guess. The other guys don't much like
> girls hangin round with us.

This passage, which reminds the reader of where the protagonist is and what he is doing, demonstrates a concept I call *keeping the reader in the scene.*

If you're telling your story through the perceptions of a protagonist, you might forget to occasionally remind them of what the scene looks like and what is happening in the scene.

Another thing writers often forget to do is make sure the reader "sees" every scene clearly. Writers often have the details of a scene in their minds, but they may forget to get those details down on the paper. I call that the *in the writer's head* problem. It's one of the most challenging issues in fiction: every writer, be it a beginning writer or a very advanced writer, struggles with how to make sure the reader sees a scene they way they see it.

Point-of-view descriptions are the best solution to that problem. It doesn't take many extra words to turn standard "restaurant" into a low-cost pizza joint that smells (to the protagonist) like burnt cheese.

By having our protagonist stand up and throw the clam shells hard, it not only keeps the reader in the scene, it also characterizes him.

I also used the sound of the flying clam shells to trigger a memory about his little sister (she hummed to herself when she was happy, which she wasn't very often). It becomes yet another clue about what might have really happened to her.

With this, the story now has some elements of *a mystery*. The mother thinks the girl drowned herself in the river, but did she? As the reader learns more about the girl, will they think she is the type of person who would commit suicide by jumping into the river?

By having our protagonist think about what type of person his little sister was, the reader gets to vicariously participate in the process of solving the mystery of her disappearance.

Let's continue that kind of protagonist thought to provide the reader with more information about her.

> **But she wasn't much for hangin round anyhow. When she didn't have chores to do, I never saw her bein with anybody else. I guess she just liked bein alone. Don't know why. Couple a times, I saw her comin back from the woods all alone. I wonder why she liked to go out there in them dark woods all by herself. Funny, at the time I didn't think much about it. Now I'm wonderin.**

Now that the reader has a better idea of who the girl was (a moody loner) will it make the reader more, or less, certain she actually did drown herself?

My plan is to keep that question in front of the reader throughout (it is the *golden thread of plot* that is always noticeable within the overall fabric of this story).

Some writers might try to characterize the girl and her relationship with her brother by providing the reader with a *flashback* scene from the past. But that would be an interruption of the chronological sequence of story events.

There are two reasons to avoid full-fledged flashbacks in a short story. First of all, it takes the reader "out" of the ongoing story, possibly losing the reader's vicarious involvement that we worked so hard to establish. Secondly, readers may not read as carefully as we hope they will, and unless you can create very good transitions into and out of the flashback, readers might miss the transition into the flashback and be confused about how the flashback scene fits into the ongoing story.

The solution is to use *memory* instead of flashback. When the boy *remembers* how his sister didn't seem to have friends and how she used to go for walks by herself in the dark woods, the reader is provided with backstory information about the girl, even though they are still *within* the current perceptions of the boy.

Even if you use memory rather than flashback to provide the reader with backstory, it's always a good idea to have the memory triggered by a story event.

In this case, the sound of the flying punched-out shells reminds him of his sister's humming.

Now, let's bring the reader out of the memory and back to the ongoing scene by having him once again notice what the sheriff's boat is doing.

> **The sheriff's boat has been goin back and forth for a long time, and they haven't snagged her up yet. I wonder how long they'll keep tryin. I'm startin to wonder if maybe she's not really down there under all that water, even if ma did get her hard feelin about it.**

The main purpose of this paragraph is to bring the reader back to the story's main scene, the dragging of the river, but I still make sure to include a *two step* in the form of character thought. *Step one* is his observation of a story event (the boat going back and forth), and *step two* is his sudden thought that if they don't find her, it might mean his sister *is not* in the river.

About this time, the reader might be wondering what the other people in the town are doing. Let's deal with that.

> **I guess the word is out about what the sheriff is up to, cause more and more people are showin up down-river from me to watch the draggin. The womenfolk are gathered together on the little patch of grass where the main street ends at the edge of the river, and the menfolk are all standing out on the dock behind Herb's fishin supplies store.**

Here, I've brought some walk-on characters into the story to represent the townspeople.

They are not described in any detail, but I do describe where they are *relative to the protagonist*. Once again, it clearly establishes him as an outsider. Let's continue to build on that idea.

> **Nobody comes near to where I'm sittin on the riverbank. I guess they don't know what to say to me, or maybe the idea of her bein out there under that muddy water scares them some. Whatever they're thinkin, they stick close together, the women in their group on the grass by the water and the men in their group out on Herb's dock. Nobody is sayin much.**

This keeps the reader *in the scene* by revealing that the people are clustered together *and* keeping their distance from our protagonist.

At this point in a story, some writers might bring in a *plot complication*. Should we do that? Or is it time for a *plot twist*?

TIP:

In *a character-driven story*, a **plot complication** is something that challenges the protagonist, something that threatens to keep the protagonist from accomplishing his or her goals. Romances, for example, are filled with plot complications; just when it looks like the hero is about to get the girl, some new challenge pops up to make it seem all but impossible.

On the other hand, a **plot twist** is created by adding a new and unexpected element to the story.

In this story, adding some kind of challenge for our protagonist to overcome doesn't seem appropriate. However, we are subtly developing something that could turn into *subplot*.

The unusual environment—a backwater, semi-rural town next to one of the biggest rivers in the world—is bound to have an effect on the people who live there.

TIP:

A story's **subplot** is a secondary aspect of the plot that supports and enriches the main plot. It is sometimes referred to as the "B story."

The tricky thing about developing subplots is that they are "beneath the surface" of the main storyline.

Think of it as the "between the lines" story, associations and implications that continue to crop up during the progression of the story but are never dealt with overtly, maybe not until the very end of the story.

One way to create a plot twist is to bring a new character onto the stage. The new character can represent the town's reaction to the river dragging and add a new element to the story. But what kind people would choose to live in a little deteriorating river town that no longer has its manufacturing base?

Every town must have its leaders or its heroes, so let's bring a "hero" into the story. The new character may temporarily take center stage, but we should bring him into the story in a way that makes it clear he is in a supporting cast role.

> **As the sheriff's boat goes puttin past Herb's fishin supplies store, I see a big guy come out of the store to stand on the dock.**
>
> **I stop throwin clam shells and watch him.**
>
> **For a while, he just watches the sheriff's boat slowly go by, and then he goes farther out onto the saggin old wooden dock to get a closer look. He's got his hand up in the air to shade his eyes from the sun. What's he up to? Why isn't he stayin with the other men at the fishin store to talk about the draggin?**
>
> **I decide to walk down there to get a closer look.**

So far, our protagonist is not sure who the big guy is. It's not a bad idea to hold off the identification of a new character for a bit; it builds a bit of suspense. Because this new character is the only person our protagonist has paid any close attention to, the reader will assume he is going to be important to the story.

> **As I get closer, I realize who the guy is. It's the catfish wranglin champ! Man, I never realized how big and fat he is. But bein big and fat don't stop him from winnin the prize for draggin out the biggest catfish**

> **every year. Catfish Wranglin Day, if you don't know
> it, is the one day of the year when Herb's fishin sup-
> plies store gives away a prize to whichever good ol boy
> can hold his breath the longest and crawl way back in
> under them muddy backwater riverbanks to drag cat-
> fish out. But the winner's not the one who drags out
> the most catfish, it's the one who gets the biggest.**

Now that I've brought the concept of the catfish wrangling contest into the story, let's provide some backstory to make it a more personal issue for our protagonist.

> **Now that I'm fifteen, I'm old enough to enter the
> catfish wranglin contest myself. But I'm not gonna do
> it because I tried it a while back, and I didn't like it
> one bit. I wanted to be the next catfish wranglin
> champ myself, so I snuck off by myself to give it a try
> when nobody was around to see me do it. Right off the
> bat, I didn't like how pitch dark it was under that
> riverbank and how hard it was to hold your breath for
> that long. And I especially didn't like how the mud
> flows all around you when it gets all stirred up and
> after a while it gets to feelin like that mud is like real
> thick cement that's gonna get thicker and thicker til
> pretty soon it's gonna close off behind you and you'll
> never be able to get out of there. Down under the bank
> in all that muddy water, I got to thinkin about what if
> I got trapped in there with them big ugly catfishes. I
> know those old catfishes really will eat you as soon as
> you are dead because my daddy told me so.**

Assuming our readers are now vicariously involved with the protagonist, we've given them the feeling of what it's like to be under the water, potentially trapped.

Hopefully, they will also relate that to the idea of the sister being trapped under the water of the Mississippi.

At some level, the reader should "get" the *symbolism* of the darkness of the catfish lair.

TIP:

Symbolism is the use of symbols to bring new ideas or concepts into a story. Like many other issues in fiction, whether symbolism works the way the writer intended resides in the eye of the beholder (the reader). It's up to you, the writer, to make it work.

Symbolism can be subtle or obvious. Subtle symbols may not be recognized by the reader for what they are, while obvious symbols can fall flat if they reveal the heavy hand of the writer.

One effective way to bring symbolism into a story is to have your protagonist perceive something as symbolic. I call that *character-driven symbolism*. In my novel, **My Vietnam War**, the protagonist tries to be optimistic by thinking about the nightly mortar attacks on his firebase as a game of chance. He thinks about how many square feet of surface are in a firebase that could be hit by a falling mortar as compared to the small area he occupies. He sees it as symbolic of the larger game of chance every soldier in war participates in, where life and death are often determined by some chance happening.

The protagonist's thoughts give the reader a little more information about the contest, and more importantly, how he feels about it. The memory characterizes him, revealing that although he respects both his father and the catfish wrangling champ, he has no interest in emulating them. He secretly tried catfish wrangling himself and didn't like it. It scared him so much he knows he is not going to be an achiever in that realm.

This set of remembered events is intended to enhance the coming-of-age aspect of the plot: he is emerging into manhood, but he doesn't seem to share the values of the men in the town. Maybe he is starting to see himself as more like his sister than he thought (neither he nor his sister have found a way to fit into the town).

The boy's thoughts about catfish wrangling are obviously tied to his thoughts about his fragile young sister who may lie dead at the bottom of the river. He may not think about it directly, but at some level, he is tying his fear of being trapped underwater and being eaten by fish to thoughts about his sister who may right now be trapped down there in the darkness at the bottom of the big river (the opening line of the story described how muddy the river is in springtime).

Now let's continue to have our protagonist think about his father and catfish wrangling.

My daddy told me the trick to catfish wranglin was to take in a big breath and hold it while you crawl in under the bank feelin with your hands for a big ol lazy catfish that will just be layin in there doin nothin. He said they just lay under that muddy bank waitin for worms and bugs and dead stuff to get sucked into their big old mouths every time they breathe in. He said that once you feel one of them big old fellas, you gotta give him your whole arm so he'll bite it. He said that big ol catfish won't chew on your arm, he'll just clamp down on it real hard and hold on. That's when you're supposed to pull him out.

I asked him what happens if the catfish is too big and you can't pull him out.

He laughed and said, "Well, then the fish eats you cause he ain't never gonna let go your arm, that's for damn sure."

Anyhow, tryin it for myself made me appreciate how good the catfish wrangling champ must be to be able to pull out the biggest catfish every single year.

The father is a new off-stage character. He is introduced to the reader through protagonist memory.

Even the dialogue, the first I've used in this story, are relayed to the reader through protagonist memory.

The reader should now begin to wonder how the father is going to play into the story. Is it *foreshadowing*, or just backstory?

TIP:
Foreshadowing is a way of tipping off the reader
about something that may happen later in the story.
Foreshadowing can be subtle, or it can be direct. You
can *hint* that something is going to happen later in the
story (which builds reader interest by leaving the
future open and unpredictable), or you can simply *tell*
the reader what is going to happen later in the story
(which builds anticipation).

Now that we've introduced the father, let's provide a little more
backstory about him and the family.

> **I been goin to the Catfish Wranglin Day every year
> since I was five. That was the first time my daddy let
> me go along. He'd entered the contest that year cause
> the prize was a brand new Winchester Model 12 shot-
> gun. My daddy said we would eat good on them catfish
> for a while even if he didn't win the shotgun. He said
> he wanted to win that shotgun so he could use it to
> shoot squirrels for us to eat because that Model 12 was
> accurate as hell and squirrels weren't so bad to eat if
> you're careful and don't bite down too hard and hit
> one of them shotgun pellets and break a tooth.**

This memory not only provides the reader with more information
about the catfish wrangling contest, it also provides some information
about the father and the family's situation (the father was worrying
about how to get food for the family).

Let's continue the backstory memory.

> **But he didn't win, and it was pretty soon after that
> when he took off. My ma told me I was almost six
> when he took off for California. I got mad the day he
> said he was goin, and I even cried some in my room
> while ma was out there in the kitchen yellin at him.
> She said he was a son of a bitch for not even stickin**

> around to wait until after my six-year birthday party.
>   After he and Mama got finished with their yelling,
> Daddy came into my room and kneeled down in front
> of me to tell me he was real sorry, but he had to go
> now cause he'd been lucky enough to catch a ride in a
> big truck that was gonna take him all the way out to
> California. He told me he'd bring us all out there to
> California soon as he found a job. But he never did
> send for us. He didn't even write to us or nothin. Ma
> says he's surely six feet under by now, probably shot
> dead in one of those damn poker games he liked so
> much, or maybe he just found somebody he liked bet-
> tern us.

This backstory about the father's leaving the family is again presented to the reader through protagonist memory. As I said earlier, it's
usually better to use memory than create a full flashback scene from
the past.

Next, let's show what the protagonist thinks about his father now.

> Thinkin about it now, if he is still alive, I think it's a
> real shame that he won't ever know what happened to
> his little girl. She was hardly morn a baby when he
> left.

Now, by moving our protagonist back into his usual role of reporting to the reader, we can bring his mother back into the story.

> Ma says after all these years I might just as well
> forget about him, and I've tried, but I can't do it.

Will the reader now think there is a possibility that the father
might return? Later, we can use this concept of a missing father out
there somewhere in the world as part of the character-driven plot.

Now, it's time to create a clear transition to bring the reader back
from these backstory memories.

> **By the time I get close to the dock, the catfish wran-glin champ is wadin into the river. He's already got his pants off, and he pulls off his shirt and hangs it over edge of the dock. Man, he's got a big belly. It hangs way out over the waist of his long underwear.**

Through our protagonist's perception, we are gradually giving the reader more and more information about this new character.

As the annual top-prize winner at Catfish Wranglin Day, he is clearly one of the more famous people in the town. The protagonist, like everyone else in town, is quite impressed with the man because of his one notable accomplishment, his ability to go down under the water and pull giant catfish out from under a muddy bank.

But how is that one accomplishment going to play into this situation? So far, all the reader knows about what this new character looks like is his weight. I'm only describing physical attributes of a charac-ter if it's going to be relevant to the story, so how is weight going to play into this story?

> **He wades in deeper and deeper. When he's clear in up to his shoulders, he puts some kind of metal clamp on his nose, takes one last look back at the group of men back at the fishin supplies store, and starts to swim out. He keeps on swimmin til he's out past the end of the dock, and that's where the strong current starts to pull him downstream. He doesn't even try to fight it. He just takes in a great big breath and ducks down under the water.**
>
> **I know right away what he's gonna do. He's gonna go down and find Sis on the bottom of that big old river.**

At this point in the story, the protagonist is in the role of observer. He is close enough to the action to see what is going on, but he is not involved.

That's because I don't want him to be involved; in this charac-ter-driven story, I want him to think of himself as an outsider and be motivated by that.

> **The men hurry out onto the dock to watch.**
> **"He's gonna go down and get her," says one old**
> **dried-up guy.**
> **Another old guy says, "By God, he can probly do er**
> **too if he sets his mind to it."**
> **But a third old guy says, "Aw hell, she's probly**
> **washed all the way down to Keithsburg by now, or**
> **maybe even clear down to Oquawka." He won't find**
> **hide nor hair a her.**

The purpose of creating the set of onlookers is to show their diverse opinions about the chances of success for the catfish wrangler. I'm using *dialogue* to do it so the reader can "listen in" while the locals discuss what's happening.

TIP:

The **eavesdropping technique** is when you create dialogue exchanges between the characters in the story in order to put readers in the role of *eaves-droppers*. They learn what is going on in the story by "listening in" on what the characters in the story are saying.

Unfortunately, in character-driven stories, your protagonist will often be alone, which rules out the use of the eavesdropping technique. Unless, that is, you want to make your protagonist schizophrenic. In two of my novels, **Psalm for Cock Robin** and **The Pain Artist**, my protagonist has "another self" to talk to even when he is alone. That gave me a way to use the dialogue tool in many different situations so my readers could "**eavesdrop**" on the imagined conversations of my loner protagonist.

By having the old men who hang around the fishing supplies story discuss the extraordinary capabilities of the catfish wrangler, I've created *motivation* for the catfish wrangler's actions. Presumably, the ego of the renowned catfish wrangling chap is not going to let him just stand by while the sheriff fails at finding the young girl's body.

He will heroically swim out and find her himself.

This brings a new plot element into the story: can the catfish wrangler actually find the girl even if the sheriff and his deputy can't? Does his prowess at going underwater to get the biggest catfish every year, mean he really *is* some kind of underwater superhero?

I've made *some* of the older men of the town sure he will succeed, simply because he *is* the catfish wranglin champ.

None of them seem to doubt it, unless it's too late and the girl has been washed downriver.

But will the reader believe it? Maybe they won't be so sure. To enhance the drama, let's keep the question open for a bit while we convey what our protagonist is thinking about the situation.

> **If Sis *is* out there under all that water, I'm hopin the catfish wrangler *really can* find her. I mean, if he can crawl under them muddy banks and hold his breath for long enough to get ahold of a big old catfish and drag it out, maybe he just might be able to go all the way down to the bottom of the river and get ahold my little sister. Even though it would mean she really is dead, it'd be better than if the sheriff snags her with those terrible sharp treble-hooks.**

Here, I've given our protagonist the hope that if his sister really is out there under the water, the catfish wrangler will find her. The reader should now understand that he has doubts about the catfish wrangler's chances, but he is trying to share the hopes of the other townspeople who believe in the man.

It relates to the continuing theme of "fitting in." Will he join with the other men of the town and go to join them on the dock? Or will he continue to stand back and observe, even though it is his sister that the catfish wrangler is searching for?

> **I wait to see how long it'll be before he comes up again.**
> **None of the men are talkin now.**
> **One of them mumbles somethin I don't catch.**
> **I look at the their faces. They seem worried. Are they thinking he's been under the water too long?**

> **But I've seen the catfish wrangler hold his breath longer than this. Every year, he stays down under those muddy banks until he finds the biggest catfish, no matter how long it takes.**

Our protagonist, still in the role of "outsider," looks at the faces of the "insiders" to try to discern what they are thinking.

The reader should also be "seeing" their worries. It *foreshadows* what is going to happen next.

> **But pretty soon, one of the old men scratches his gray beard and says, "Aw, now nobody can hold their breath *that* long."**
>
> **But another old man, who doesn't have a beard, shakes his finger at the first guy and says, "Sure he can. He can do er. You just wait an see."**
>
> **As we wait for him to come back up, I keep on remindin myself that this man is the catfish wranglin champ. He can hold his breath like almost forever. He'll come back up soon, and maybe he'll have Sis in his arms.**

Now that the sheriff and his deputy don't seem to be able to find the girl's body, the men of the town, including our protagonist, have placed their faith in the abilities of the catfish wrangler. Does it mean that if the catfish wrangler can't find the girl, they will have to face the fact that she's gone?

Although our protagonist is still holding out hope that the catfish wrangler will find his sister's body, will the reader have as much faith in the man?

The dialogue, and the worry on the faces of the men, is revealing doubt. The issue creating the doubt is time: how long has the catfish wrangler been under the water, and how long can *any* man actually hold his breath? In this scene, in which the onlookers are doing nothing but watching, how do we convey *the concept of time passing*. By having the supporting-cast characters *discuss* how much time is passing, we should be able to convince the reader that the catfish wrangler has been under the water too long and may be in trouble.

A fiction writer must successfully create a *diegetic universe*, a world that exists within the story, and one important aspect of that diegetic universe is time passing. The issue of time passing in fiction is a complex one. Within the world of the story, things happen and people talk. In the reader's mind, that uses up time.

A common writing mistake is to be unaware of how the reader is going to perceive the passage of time within the story. It's another one of those "in the writer's head" issues; that is, the writer may think they "know" how much time has passed in the story, but they fail to convey the time concept to the reader. They may want the reader to accept that a large amount of time has passed, but they write only a few words to describe the events in the scene. The reader, having read only a few words, may feel like only a short amount of time has passed.

So, how does a writer convey time passing? There are many methods, including the most obvious, using the narrative role to "tell" the reader that time has passed. Narrative phrases like "After an hour," or "Later that day," or "The next morning," all convey time passing, but it leaves the protagonist out of the story. It becomes a narrator passing information to the reader.

You *could* have someone in the scene check their watch, but there are more subtle methods, such as creating story events that take time to play out. A scene in which an entire meal is consumed or a great distance has been traveled requires a fair amount of time. And a scene that starts in broad daylight and ends in darkness also shows that a considerable amount of time has passed.

However, those kinds of methods won't work in every scene. In that case, you can always use protagonist thought about time passing, and/or have the other characters in the story *refer* to time passing.

In this case, we can use *the eavesdropping technique*: the reader can "listen to" the characters in the scene discuss how much time has passed since the catfish wrangler went down under the water.

The catfish wrangler's actions have brought the story to a tipping point. We now have a capable swimmer under the water who seems to be having trouble dealing with the power of the mighty river. The assumption is, if he can't handle the power of the river, what chance does a little girl have?

It brings home the concept of how different the two worlds of the story are: the world of land and sky is knowable and understandable, while the underwater world is dark and mysterious and fearful.

The earlier scene in which our protagonist explored the silent darkness of the catfish lair showed the reader the potential danger of being under the water.

Now the men of the town are confronting the possibility that even the most skilled of them may not be able to master the dark and dangerous world that is beneath the muddy water.

It's time to let the reader know the outcome. Let's do it using a combination of protagonist thought and showing the reactions of the supporting-cast characters.

> **But he doesn't come up.**
> **I don't know how much time has passed, but I'm startin to think it's been too long a time for a human person to be holdin their breath, even if he is the catfish wranglin champ.**
> **Everybody's lookin at each other like they can't believe what's happening.**

Through the use of both dialogue and narration, we have indicated to the reader that too much time has passed, and therefore, the catfish wrangler is in trouble. If the catfish wrangler is not going to come up, the story suddenly shifts to a new issue: if the mighty river has now taken the life of the catfish wrangler, for the townspeople at least, it is a much more significant event than the disappearance of a loner girl at the edge of this community.

Now, we need to show how the townspeople, including the sheriff, would react to such a calamity.

> **It's strange, but nobody says anything. They don't even seem to want to look at each other.**
> **The terrible silence continues until the sheriff's boat goes puttin by. Then all them men start yellin and wavin.**
> **The deputy pulls the boat in next to the dock and shuts off the motor.**
> **"What the hell's the matter with you people?" says the sheriff. "What's all the yellin about?"**
> **The old men are all excited and pointin out toward the river, all of em talkin at once, tellin the sheriff that**

> **the catfish wranglin champ went down lookin for the girl and never came back up.**
>
> **The sheriff turns to look at where they're pointin. He shakes his head and says, "Damn. Why'd he hafta go and do a fool thing like that?" Then he turns to his deputy and says, "Well, we'd better go get him fore he gets too far downstream."**

Here, I'm using a combination of narration and dialogue to portray the scene. There is no specific rule about when to use dialogue, but in this kind of scene, I like to mix dialogue ("What the hell's the matter with you people?") with narrator-summarized speech (The old men are all excited and pointin out toward the river, all of em talkin at once).

Because the sheriff is a character that's been identified earlier, I decided to give him actual words. I just used the narrator to summarize what the other non-identified characters were saying.

> **The deputy starts up the motor and swings the boat downstream. The boat is movin fast with the sheriff standin up in the back workin the drag lines.**
>
> **It isn't long before the sheriff yells somethin, and the deputy shuts off the motor.**
>
> **The sheriff starts pullin at one of the wires. Whatever he's caught, it looks heavy.**
>
> **The deputy turns the boat around and points it upstream. He throttles down the motor til the boat is all but standin still out there. Then they're both at the back of the boat pullin on the wire.**

This scene is all point-of-view description. Through the perceptions of the protagonist, the reader is given access to the action of the scene.

> **Pretty soon, they get ahold of somethin that looks like a big leg. I can see that the leg has got one of them terrible big treble hooks stuck deep into it.**

I'm keeping the reader in the scene by describing what the sheriff is doing and how the deputy is handling the boat. And then, by describing what they get hold of as "a leg," a *part* of a human body, I'm trying to convey the stark lifelessness of a dead body.

> **It doesn't take em long before they get ahold of the other leg and pull the body up into the boat. Sure enough, it's the catfish wranglin champ, and it looks like he's all tangled up in fishin lines that have lots of little hooks all along em. Must be them illegal trotlines people throw out in the night to catch bullheads.**
>
> **Once they get the catfish wrangler laid out on his back, I can see that his eyes are open, like he's starin up at the sky. He's still got that metal clip on his nose, and he's got one of them sucker fish attached to his big belly. The sheriff tears off the sucker fish and cracks it on the side of the boat to kill it. He throws the dead fish back into the water, and the deputy speeds the boat's motor back up.**
>
> **As they come putt-puttin back up toward the dock, all the men crowd around.**

Because I want the story to start moving toward a conclusion, I described the finding of the man rather quickly.

I generally like to start my stories at a leisurely pace, then, once the reader is invested in the character, the setting, and the situation, I try to quicken the pace as I bring the story to a conclusion.

Now that the body of the catfish wrangler has been recovered, the story seems to have turned from a search for a young girl, a loner who has no real role in the town, to a catastrophe in which one of the most notable citizens of the town has drowned while attempting to play the role of a hero. Our protagonist knows the townspeople; he knows they are no longer interested in his sister's disappearance.

> **I can see they're gonna be the rest of the day takin care of the catfish wrangler's body. I guess they forgot all about findin my little sister, so I head home to tell ma they didn't find her.**
>
> **As I go, I kick at pebbles on the road, raisin up dust**

and thinkin that since the sheriff didn't find her and she didn't get tangled up in any of those illegal trot lines, maybe ma is wrong. Maybe my little sister isn't at the bottom of that big ol river after all. Maybe she just left this dumb ol town. Maybe she mighta even gone out to California to find Daddy. I seen the way some men look at her since she started to fill out under that thin old dress she wears. Maybe some man took a likin to her and offered to give her a ride all the way out to California. Hell, maybe by now she's half the way out there.

As I walk, I'm thinkin maybe that's what I should do too. One of these days, I could just up and disappear, and then they'd be out there draggin the river for me. But the joke would be on them. I wouldn't be down there under the water gettin et by them big old catfish. I'd be long, long gone, on my way to California.

The story concludes with our protagonist coming up with an explanation of his sister's disappearance that differs from his mother's. That indicates he is becoming more of his own person.

TIP:

How a protagonist changes over the course of the story is known as **character arc**. It's often the most demonstrable aspect of plot in these kinds of character-driven, coming-of-age stories. The arc evolves as the protagonist learns new life lessons. In a character-driven story, the protagonist starts out with a baseline set of behaviors and/or beliefs, but the situation and the unfolding story events affect that person until, by the end of the story, the character's behaviors and/or beliefs will have changed (for better or for worse).

In a novel, character arc usually evolves through exposure to many different experiences, but in a short story, the evolution of the character will usually be less gradual and will be closely tied to one situation.

Many writers understand that a character needs to have grown by the end of the story, but they fail to "get inside" the protagonist's mind to show the reader how the events of the story gradually brought about that change. Instead, they may try to use the narrative role to "tell" the reader that the character has changed. That will fall flat. Readers don't want to be *told* about character arc, they want to "see" it evolving.

In this story, the ending is designed to tell the reader that our protagonist is now thinking about potential alternatives to living out his life in this small river town. The implication is that he must take some kind of action to avoid eventually becoming like the old men who hang around the fishing supplies store.

Except for his kicking pebbles on the road, which I inserted simply to *keep the reader in the scene*, the conclusion to the story is all about the protagonist's thoughtful analysis of the situation. He reviews what has happened and makes a decision about what it all means. For the vicariously-involved reader, it should be a satisfactory ending for this kind of character-driven story.

Review

Below is a reprint of the completed story. As you review the story, look for the fiction-writing techniques we explored in this chapter, including:

- Developing an opening scene that conveys the most **important elements of the locale** and is **representative of the environment** in which the majority of the story events will take place.

- Introducing the reader to the world of the story through **protagonist perception** to create **vicarious involvement** with the protagonist.

- Putting the protagonist in the **role of reporter**, one who is **observant and thoughtful**.

- Establishing the protagonist's storytelling "**voice**."

- Sometimes using **sentence fragments** to convey the "feel" of **character thought**.

- Relaying information about **the situation** through **protagonist thought**.

- **Characterizing the protagonist** by showing how he "sees" the world of the story.

- Sticking to **one point of view** unless you have a **good reason** to do otherwise.

- Getting the reader vicariously involved with the protagonist through the use of the action/reaction **two-step**.

- Creating **clear transitions** into and out of **protagonist memories**.

- Creating story events that are related to the protagonist's **need to respond to the situation** (if only through thought and decision-making).

- Creating a **world of the story** for the reader, including making the reader aware of **the passage of time**.

- Providing the reader with information (through protagonist perception) about the **supporting-cast characters**.

- Making sure each of the **supporting-cast characters**—although they may be unnamed—has a **specific role** in the story.

- Making sure **supporting-cast characters** are described in terms of their **role in the story** rather than who they might be as individual persons.

- Keeping the reader **in the scene**.

- Avoiding scene details that don't characterize or are **not relevant** to the ongoing story.

- Avoiding **telling** the story using a narrator instead of **showing** story events through the perceptions of the protagonist.

- Providing the reader with story-related events that occurred before the time frame of the story (**backstory**) through the use of **protagonist memory, triggered by a story event,** rather than through the use of **flashback**.

- Avoiding story **dilution** by providing only story information that is relevant to the story.

- Getting significant story events and scene details down on the paper in a way **the reader** can "see" them (i.e. avoiding the "**in the writer's head**" problem).

- Using **symbolism** to bring new ideas or concepts into the story

- Using **foreshadowing** to tip off the reader that a new story event or a new supporting-cast character may eventually play an important role in the story.

- Using **dialogue** and the **eavesdropping technique** to provide story information to the reader.

The Darkness of the Catfish Lair

If my little sister woulda gone under the mighty Mississippi River durin the fall, or even when the winter is just startin to come on and the patches of thin silvery ice get to spreadin across the backwater shallows, they mighta been able to see her body down there on the bottom just by lookin down into the water usin their bottom-looker, that tube they got with the glass in the end of it.

But in the late springtime, like it is now, the big ol Missip is near in flood stage and the water gets so muddy you can't even see your hand when you stick it in up to the elbow. When the river gets that muddy, they hafta drag for the bodies.

This mornin, when the sheriff and his deputy were gettin ready to start draggin the river, I saw em tyin some long wires to the back end of their old wood boat. Then they tied some big ol sharp and real mean-lookin treble-hooks onto the ends of them wires.

Now, as I'm sittin here on the riverbank watchin em go back and forth, first upstream and then back down again, with the sheriff standin up at the back of the boat keepin the drag lines from gettin all tangled up, I try not to think about those sharp hooks too much. I don't want to even imagine what those sharp things would do to her soft little body if they do snag her up.

Even though she was only a year younger than me, she was a little thing. Not tall and gangly like me. Ma always says the two of us are so different it's hard to believe we both came out of her. But we do both got the same blonde hair, even though mine is getting darker as I get older. Unlike me, she had a sort of softness to her, ever since she was little. Softness in her bein too.

Maybe that's why ma thinks she probly went and threw herself in the river.

The sheriff told ma that maybe we oughta hold off on the draggin for a bit cause the girl'd only been gone the one day. But ma told him she'd got a hard feelin that her little girl is down under that muddy ol water.

What with ma thinkin Sis is out there drowned in the river, I didn't go to school today. I just been sittin here on the riverbank all mornin watchin the draggin.

The sheriff's old boat takes on water some, and the boat motor is pretty weak, so they don't hardly make any progress goin upstream against the current. But once they get a ways upstream, they get their boat turned around and shut off the motor so they can just float downstream until they get to the sandbar that's all the way down almost to Linden's bend. I guess they figure if she didn't get caught on the river bottom or hung up on that sandbar, she'll be long gone down the river to who knows where.

Every time they get their boat floated down to the sandbar, the deputy has to pull the motor's starter cord a bunch of times, cussin and cussin, til he finally gets it goin again, and then they come putt-puttin their way back up here again.

While I watch em go draggin back and forth, I pass the time by throwin punched-out clam shells at the water. Them punched-out clam shells are layin all over the place. Piles of em, left over from the old pearl button factory that's been closed since even before I was born. Don't know why the factory closed down. No clams left in this ol river, I guess. Some say all them clams got done in by oil that leaks out of the oil barges that pass by here day and night. Maybe so, maybe not. It could just be that the button factory caught so many clams there weren't none left.

I stand up and toss them punched-out shells out into the river as far as I can. If I throw 'em hard enough, the holes in those shells make a whistlin sound as they fly out over the water. It's kind of a lonesome sound, and it makes me think of how Sis always liked to hum songs to herself while she was out all alone in the garden doin her hoein. I get kind of sad rememberin her when she was hummin like that. I think maybe her hummin like that meant she was at least a little bit happy, which she wasn't very often.

Another reason I throw em so hard is cause I'm feelin kinda mad. If she really is out there drowned, and they drag her body up, I'm gonna get even madder cause maybe I coulda done somethin to prevent it. Maybe I coulda played with her more, or at least talked to her more. I don't know why I didn't. Cause she was a girl I guess. The other guys don't much like girls hangin round with us.

But she wasn't much for hangin round anyhow. When she didn't have chores to do, I never saw her bein with anybody else. I guess she just liked bein alone. Don't know why. Couple a times, I saw her comin back from the woods all alone. I wonder why she liked to go out there in them dark woods all by herself. Funny, at the time I didn't think much about it. Now I'm wonderin.

The sheriff's boat has been goin back and forth for a long time, and they haven't snagged her up yet. I wonder how long they'll keep tryin. I'm startin to wonder if maybe she's not really down there under all that water, even if ma did get her hard feelin about it.

I guess the word is out about what the sheriff is up to, cause more and more people are showin up downriver from me to watch the draggin. The womenfolk are gathered together on the little patch of grass where the main street ends at the edge of the river, and the menfolk are all standing out on the dock behind Herb's fishin supplies store.

Nobody comes near to where I'm sittin on the riverbank. I guess they don't know what to say to me, or maybe the idea of her bein out there under that muddy water scares them some. Whatever they're thinkin, they stick close together, the women in their group on the grass by the water and the men in their group out on Herb's dock. Nobody is sayin much.

As the sheriff's boat goes puttin past Herb's fishin supplies store, I see a big guy come out of the store to stand on the dock.

I stop throwin clam shells and watch him.

For a while, he just watches the sheriff's boat slowly go by, and then he goes farther out onto the saggin old wooden dock to get a closer look. He's got his hand up in the air to shade his eyes from the sun. What's he up to? Why isn't he stayin with the other men at the fishin store to talk about the draggin?

I decide to walk down there to get a closer look.

As I get closer, I realize who the guy is. It's the catfish wranglin champ! Man, I never realized how big and fat he is. But bein big and fat don't stop him from winnin the prize for draggin out the biggest catfish every year. Catfish Wranglin Day, if you don't know it, is the one day of the year when Herb's fishin supplies store gives away a prize to whichever good ol boy can hold his breath the longest and crawl way back in under them muddy backwater riverbanks to drag catfish out. But the winner's not the one who drags out the most catfish, it's the one who gets the biggest.

Now that I'm fifteen, I'm old enough to enter the catfish wranglin contest myself. But I'm not gonna do it because I tried it a while back, and I didn't like it one bit. I wanted to be the next catfish wranglin champ myself, so I snuck off by myself to give it a try when nobody was around to see me do it. Right off the bat, I didn't like how pitch dark it was under that riverbank and how hard it was to hold your breath for that long. And I especially didn't like how the mud flows all around you when it gets all stirred up and after a while it gets to feelin like that mud is like real thick cement that's gonna get thicker and thicker til pretty soon it's gonna close off behind you and you'll never be able to get out of there. Down under the bank in all that muddy water, I got to thinkin about what if I got trapped in there with them big ugly catfishes. I know those old catfishes really will eat you as soon as you are dead because my daddy told me so.

My daddy told me the trick to catfish wranglin was to take in a big breath and hold it while you crawl in under the bank feelin with your hands for a big ol lazy catfish that will just be layin in there doin nothin. He said they just lay under that muddy bank waitin for worms and bugs and dead stuff to get sucked into their big old mouths every time they breathe in. He said that once you feel one of them big old fellas, you gotta give him your whole arm so he'll bite it. He said that big ol catfish won't chew on your arm, he'll just clamp down on it real hard and hold on. That's when you're supposed to pull him out.

I asked him what happens if the catfish is too big and you can't pull him out.

He laughed and said, "Well, then the fish eats you cause he ain't never gonna let go your arm, that's for damn sure."

Anyhow, tryin it for myself made me appreciate how good the catfish wrangling champ must be to be able to pull out the biggest catfish every single year.

I been goin to the Catfish Wranglin Day every year since I was five. That was the first time my daddy let me go along. He'd entered the contest that year cause the prize was a brand new Winchester Model 12 shotgun. My daddy said we would eat good on them catfish for a while even if he didn't win the shotgun. He said he wanted to win that shotgun so he could use it to shoot squirrels for us to eat because that Model 12 was accurate as hell and squirrels weren't so bad to eat if you're careful and don't bite down too hard and hit one of them shotgun pellets and break a tooth.

But he didn't win, and it was pretty soon after that when he took off. My ma told me I was almost six when he took off for California. I got mad the day he said he was goin, and I even cried some in my room while ma was out there in the kitchen yellin at him. She said he was a son of a bitch for not even stickin around to wait until after my six-year birthday party.

After he and Mama got finished with their yelling, Daddy came into my room and kneeled down in front of me to tell me he was real sorry, but he had to go now cause he'd been lucky enough to catch a ride in a big truck that was gonna take him all the way out to California. He told me he'd bring us all out there to California soon as he found a job. But he never did send for us. He didn't even write to us or nothin. Ma says he's surely six feet under by now, probably shot dead in one of those damn poker games he liked so much, or maybe he just found somebody he liked bettern us.

Thinkin about it now, if he is still alive, I think it's a real shame that he won't ever know what happened to his little girl. She was hardly morn a baby when he left.

Ma says after all these years I might just as well forget about him, and I've tried, but I can't do it.

By the time I get close to the dock, the catfish wranglin champ is wadin into the river. He's already got his pants off, and he pulls off his shirt and hangs it over edge of the dock. Man, he's got a big belly. It hangs way out over the waist of his long underwear.

He wades in deeper and deeper. When he's clear in up to his shoulders, he puts some kind of metal clamp on his nose, takes one last look back at the group of men back at the fishin supplies store, and starts to swim out. He keeps on swimmin til he's out past the end of the dock, and that's where the strong current starts to pull him downstream. He doesn't even try to fight it. He just takes in a great big breath and ducks down under the water.

I know right away what he's gonna do. He's gonna go down and find Sis on the bottom of that big old river.

The men hurry out onto the dock to watch.

"He's gonna go down and get her," says one old dried-up guy.

Another old guy says, "By God, he can probly do er too if he sets his mind to it."

But a third old guy says, "Aw hell, she's probly washed all the way down to Keithsburg by now, or maybe even clear down to Oquawka." He won't find hide nor hair a her.

If Sis *is* out there under all that water, I'm hopin the catfish wrangler *really can* find her. I mean, if he can crawl under them muddy banks and hold his breath for long enough to get ahold of a big old catfish and drag it out, maybe he just might be able to go all the way down to the bottom of the river and get ahold my little sister. Even though it would mean she really is dead, it'd be better than if the sheriff snags her with those terrible sharp tre-ble-hooks.

I wait to see how long it'll be before he comes up again.

None of the men are talkin now.

One of them mumbles somethin I don't catch.

I look at the their faces. They seem worried. Are they thinking he's been under the water too long?

But I've seen the catfish wrangler hold his breath longer than this. Every year, he stays down under them muddy banks until he finds the biggest catfish, no matter how long it takes.

But pretty soon, one of the old men scratches his gray beard and says, "Aw, now nobody can hold their breath *that* long."

But another old man, who doesn't have a beard, shakes his finger at the first guy and says, "Sure he can. He can do er. You just wait an see."

As we wait for him to come back up, I keep on remindin myself that this man is the catfish wranglin champ. He can hold his breath like almost forever. He'll come back up soon, and maybe he'll have Sis in his arms.

But he doesn't come up.

I don't know how much time has passed, but I'm startin to think it's been too long a time for a human person to be holdin their breath, even if he is the catfish wranglin champ.

Everybody's lookin at each other like they can't believe what's happening.

It's strange, but nobody says anything. They don't even seem to want to look at each other.

The terrible silence continues until the sheriff's boat goes puttin by. Then all them men start yellin and wavin.

The deputy pulls the boat in next to the dock and shuts off the motor.

"What the hell's the matter with you people?" says the sheriff. "What's all the yellin about?"

The old men are all excited and pointin out toward the river, all of em talkin at once, tellin the sheriff that the catfish wranglin champ went down lookin for the girl and never came back up.

The sheriff turns to look at where they're pointin. He shakes his head and says, "Damn. Why'd he hafta go and do a fool thing like that?" Then he turns to his deputy and says, "Well, we'd better go get him fore he gets too far downstream."

The deputy starts up the motor and swings the boat downstream. The boat is movin fast with the sheriff standin up in the back workin the drag lines.

It isn't long before the sheriff yells somethin, and the deputy shuts off the motor.

The sheriff starts pullin at one of the wires. Whatever he's caught, it looks heavy.

The deputy turns the boat around and points it upstream. He throttles down the motor til the boat is all but standin still out there. Then they're both at the back of the boat pullin on the wire.

Pretty soon, they get ahold of somethin that looks like a big leg. I can see that the leg has got one of them terrible big treble hooks stuck deep into it.

It doesn't take em long before they get ahold of the other leg and pull the body up into the boat. Sure enough, it's the catfish wranglin champ, and it looks like he's all tangled up in fishin lines that have lots of little hooks all along em. Must be them illegal trotlines people throw out in the night to catch bullheads.

Once they get the catfish wrangler laid out on his back, I can see that his eyes are open, like he's starin up at the sky. He's still got that metal clip on his nose, and he's got one of them sucker fish attached to his big belly. The sheriff tears off the sucker fish and cracks it on the side of the boat to kill it. He throws the dead fish back into the water, and the deputy speeds the boat's motor back up.

As they come putt-puttin back up toward the dock, all the men crowd around.

I can see they're gonna be the rest of the day takin care of the catfish wrangler's body. I guess they forgot all about findin my little sister, so I head home to tell ma they didn't find her.

As I go, I kick at pebbles on the road, raisin up dust and thinkin that since the sheriff didn't find her and she didn't get tangled up in any of those illegal trot lines, maybe ma is wrong. Maybe my little sister isn't at the bottom of that big ol river after all. Maybe she just left this dumb ol town. Maybe she mighta even gone out to California to find Daddy. I seen the way some men look at her since she started to fill out under that thin old dress she wears. Maybe some man took a likin to her and offered to give her a ride all the way out to California. Hell, maybe by now she's half the way out there.

As I walk, I'm thinkin maybe that's what I should do too. One of these days, I could just up and disappear, and then they'd be out there draggin the river for me. But the joke would be on them. I wouldn't be down there under the water gettin et by them big old catfish. I'd be long, long gone, on my way to California.

3

Writing the Second-Person Story

Let's start right out with a statement about second-person: logically, there is no such thing as the second-person *point of view,* at least not in the way we normally think of it. There is no way to tell a story from the perspective of a second-person narrator.

However, you *can* use a *second-person pronoun* to address readers directly (you readers). You can also use a second-person pronoun to refer to everybody in general (If you live in LA, you have to get used to the traffic).

There is also a fiction-writing technique known as *metafiction* that uses second-person pronouns to intentionally draw attention to the fact that the reader is reading a work of fiction. My novel, **The Pain Artist**, uses *metafiction* to alter the traditional roles of writer and reader, often directing comments specifically to the reader (I know it's a bleak world I'm creating for you).

While there is not actually any such thing as the second-person *point of view*, there *is* such a thing as a *second-person story*. I would describe it as a story in which the protagonist refers to himself using second-person pronouns (You open your eyes. You don't recognize this room. How did you get here?). Such stories, while fairly unusual, can be an effective way to convey the concept that a first-person narrator feels estranged from himself, almost as if he is seeing himself from without. That approach focuses the reader's attention on the protagonist's state of mind, helping to make it an interesting character-driven story. In terms of actual *point of view*, the story is being told from a protagonist's *first-person perspective*, but the first-person narrator is referring to himself using the second-person pronoun "you." Let's use that approach to create a second-person story.

Getting the Story Started

In the previous chapter's example story, we began by coming up with a protagonist. Let's do that again for this story.

Because I completed a PhD in psychology and worked in mental hospitals before I began my graduate studies in creative writing, I usually write psychological novels about characters that struggle with mental issues. For example, my Vietnam War novel followed a young soldier in Vietnam as he spiraled down into PTSD. Let's use that same sort of soldier character to create a psychological story.

That also gives us our setting, Vietnam.

Earlier, I discussed the concept of narrator unreliability. To demonstrate that technique, let's make this story an **unreliable narrator** story. That means we will have to find a way to make the reader aware that the protagonist is not a reliable reporter of reality.

Story narrators can be seen as unreliable because of youth, lack of experience, or impaired mental ability. The latter could be caused by mental illness or by outside factors such as alcohol or drug intake.

Creating an unreliable narrator can enhance reader interest, but it can be tricky to pull off if you don't have an outside narrator to "tell" the reader the protagonist is unreliable. The protagonist's unreliability has to be discerned by the reader by way of the protagonist's actions and thoughts.

So, where would we start such a story? In general, short stories should be told in chronological order, unless there is *a good reason* to do otherwise.

We could start the story with our protagonist receiving his draft notice and then proceed chronologically from there as he goes through Army training and ends up being sent to Vietnam. But I would rather create a story that is *about* his experiences in Vietnam. As we saw in the last chapter, we can get that kind of *backstory* information in later by using protagonist memory.

To make our protagonist entirely naive about what it's like to be a "real" soldier, let's say he is not a combat soldier, but is instead in some kind of behind-the-lines support role (three quarters of all the soldiers who were sent to Vietnam ended up behind the front lines in a support role). Many of the support troops didn't even have to go through Advanced Individual Training and were therefore fresh from Basic Training. If our protagonist was one of that type, he would know little about soldiering and nothing about the country he was in.

Next, we need to decide *the location* of our opening scene. Many, if not most, of the soldiers who were stationed in Saigon spent a lot of their free time hanging out in the local bars. So, to start this story, let's put him in a bar scene, and put the reader "in" his mind to show what he is thinking about.

As in our first-person story, in order to make the story *character-driven*, we will want the reader to "see" the scene through the perceptions of our protagonist.

> **Back in Basic Training, they said if you get sent to a foreign country like Vietnam you should behave in a way that upholds the honor of the U.S. Army. One thing for sure, lying drunk on a dirty barroom floor in Saigon, staring up at the underside of a table, is not behaving in a way that upholds the honor of the U.S. Army.**

This opening scene informs the reader of the setting, as perceived by a somewhat incapacitated protagonist. Of course, the reader is going to wonder how he ended up lying on a floor, but for the moment, let's hold off explaining that. It's what I might lightheartedly call the "wait for it" technique, a way to momentarily build tension or drama. In an action scene, or during exchanges of dialogue, you don't want to withhold scene information, but in this case, it can help to create the feeling of an unreliable narrator who may be confused about what exactly is going on.

This opening scene not only lets the reader know about the setting and the situation, it also puts the reader *in* the character's mind.

TIP:
When you are creating a character-driven story, you will often be starting a paragraph by moving the reader "into" the protagonist's thoughts. Think of it like a **topic sentence** in expository writing, but instead of starting a paragraph with a topic sentence that notifies the reader of what the paragraph is going to be about, this type of topic sentence is used to notify the reader that the following paragraph is going to be concerned with what the protagonist is perceiving.

The reader will immediately see that the protagonist is using second-person to refer to himself. And they might already suspect that it indicates some sort of estrangement from himself. Right from this opening paragraph, the story will have an unusual "feel" because of his use of second-person.

As you can see, I decided to start this story in the middle of an ongoing situation. I could have started the story with background information, or I could have "walked" the protagonist into the situation. There is no *right* story-starting method. It depends on how much information you think the reader needs. By starting this example story *through* the perceptions of my protagonist, I'm providing the reader with information about the scene *and* information about him (the way he thinks about the scene and about his situation characterizes him).

Next, let's give our readers a little more information about the scene by letting them know what our protagonist is hearing.

> **You are hearing noise. Loud music. Loud voices. Drunken men shouting, drunken men fighting, drunken men not upholding the honor of the U.S. Army.**

I think this is all the description I will provide about the scene because that's not what the story is going to be *about*. In order to move the reader along toward the main thrust of the story, we want to keep the pacing fairly fast here at the start.

TIP:

The **pacing** of a story is determined by the *narrative style* you choose to employ. The narrator's storytelling style will determine pacing by dictating the degree of inclusiveness (what is included and what is left out).

A narrator can tell the story in a breezy way, including only the most basic of plot elements and using brief summarizing descriptions, or the narrator can proceed in a leisurely way, describing every scene in great detail.

The best approach is probably a middle ground, keeping the story moving, but providing enough information about scenes to fully engage the reader.

One of the ways in which a short story is different from a novel is that a short story has only a few central characters. I'm thinking that this second-person story should mainly involve only two people. And what is (by far) the most popular type of two-person story? Right, a romance. In a romance story, in order to create the romance plot, the two main characters should be introduced right at the beginning. Therefore, without further ado, let's introduce the other character necessary to make the story a romance, a girl.

> **A face appears. The face is looking at you. Your blurry eyes try to focus. It's a Vietnamese face. A pretty Vietnamese girl face.**

As we learned before, in a character-driven story, whenever a story event happens, we should employ the *two-step* technique during which the protagonist reacts with action, dialogue, or thought. Let's have our protagonist react both verbally and with thought.

> **"Hello, pretty girl face."**
> **Did you say that out loud?**

He speaks, and then he self-questions, still using the second-person pronoun "you." It indicates that he is so out of it that he's not even sure whether he spoke out loud or not. It's another way to convey protagonist unreliability and to indicate his estrangement from himself, as if he is seeing himself from without.

TIP:
Self-questioning is a special type of character thought that "feels" different from normal thought. It can be used to indicate confusion or disability. For example, if you want a character to seem confused, there is no better way than to have that character ask himself "Where am I?" or "How did I get here?"

Now let's bring the girl into better "focus."

> **The pretty girl face is coming closer. Is she one of the usual girls? If only you could make your eyes focus, you might recognize her. Maybe she's a new girl. If only you could make your tongue talk, you could ask her why she looks so sad.**

Although I am showing the reader the world of the story through the protagonist's perceptions, I'm making him unsure of exactly what he is seeing. It further demonstrates his level of confusion, and again, it indicates to the reader that he might well be an unreliable narrator.

Now that we've brought our main supporting-cast character, the Vietnamese girl, into the story, what shall we do with her? The fact that he's a lonely young man far from home, and we have provided him with a pretty Vietnamese girl, should have tipped off the reader that some kind of relationship is going to develop. But what kind of relationship? Our protagonist is in a bar in Vietnam in the middle of a war, and he has already described her as possibly being one of the "usual girls." Will the reader believe that the bar's amenities include prostitutes? If so, is the relationship we are implying going to be the usual one in such circumstances? We might want the reader to believe that, but of course, we don't want it to be that simple.

> **She sits down on the floor next to you.**

The girl has acted; therefore, we need to do our usual *two-step*. How about if this time, we use only character thought.

> **Sure, sit right down here, pretty girl. You can share my floor.**

It should already be clear to the reader that this Vietnamese girl is no walk-on supporting-cast type character. Let's have her continue to act and have our protagonist continue to react.

> **She takes your hand. Her hand is small. It's a delicate hand, a caring hand, a hand that wants you to be happy, to be at peace, to not be so worried all the time.**

The girl takes his hand, and I created a two-step response to that story event using protagonist thought. By having him think about her hand, we can direct the reader's attention not only to her hand, but more importantly, to *how* he thinks about her hand. He describes her hand as delicate, but goes further to interpret it as "caring." It should be clear to the reader that our unreliable narrator is interpreting data in an unrealistic way as he tries to reduce his level of worry. It provides the reader with further confirmation of some kind of mental problem, and it does so without having to use the narrative role to "tell" the reader that.

TIP:

In a character-driven story, you should be constantly watching for ways to **characterize** your protagonist. In this second-person story, we don't have the luxury of a third-person narrator to tell the reader about the character, and even if we did, that wouldn't be the best way to do it. The best approach is usually to "slip information in" as part of the protagonist's two-step responses to story events. Showing how a protagonist responds to things is one of the very best ways to characterize him.

Now, that our readers know more about the main character; it's time to give them a little more information about our other main character in this romance story, the Vietnamese girl. I don't want to switch the point of view, so I'll do that via the perceptions of the protagonist.

> **Who is this girl? Even with your blurry eyes, you can tell she's more beautiful than any girl you have seen in the entire twenty years of your wasted life. She's thin, exotic, almost dream-like in her white silk dress.**

We are conveying more information about the girl, and at the same time, providing the reader with information about the protagonist: he decides she is the most beautiful girl he has ever seen in the entire *twenty years* of his *wasted* life.

His description of the girl may be taken by the reader as somewhat unreliable (she may not actually be the most beautiful girl in the world), but they will probably trust that she really is thin, really is attractive, and really is wearing a white silk dress.

So far, I've had the girl initiate all of the action. Our protagonist has reacted mainly with thought. That should tell the reader that this particular soldier is not demonstrating the kind of aggressive male behavior that we might expect of a soldier in a bar that has already been identified as rowdy and filled with drunken men, a bar that has "usual girls." The reader may have begun to believe that our protagonist is not only an unreliable narrator but is also taken to flights of fancy (he sees her as "almost dream-like").

Our protagonist is waiting to see what the girl will do next, so let's have her do something.

> **Still holding your hand, she leans close.**
> **You feel the lightest brush of her hair against your cheek. You close your eyes. You detect the scent of . . . flowers? No, something else. But what?**

So far, I'm introducing the characters and the situation by maintaining a sort of "rhythm" that consists of story events that are followed by two-step responses from our protagonist (usually in the form of thought). To enhance the reader's vicarious involvement with him, I'm bringing in touch (lightest brush of her hair against his cheek) and his sense of smell (a vague odor—flowers?).

Okay, now that we've brought our two main characters together, what next? How about we have her do something unexpected, like telling him a story.

> **She is whispering in your ear. With the chaos of the bar all around the two of you—men drinking, men gambling, men shouting, men fighting, men not upholding the honor of the US Army—she seems to be telling you some kind of story:**
>
> "Long time ago, poor man go to forest. Family starve. He want find wood. Want trade wood for food. But when he get to forest place, wood all gone. Trees all cut down. He walk and walk, but see no tree. Then he see one tree all alone. It look like very good tree. Man very happy. He think, I cut down tree. Take back to village. Get food for family. Man get ready to hit tree with ax, but very beautiful woman come right out of air. She stand in front of

tree. She say, Stop! No cut down tree. I spirit of forest. I live in tree. Last tree left in forest. She disappear. Strange smell left behind, like flower, sweet flower man never smell before. Man drop ax and rub eyes. Did he really see spirit? Maybe he imagine her. He not want to make spirit of forest mad, but he need tree. Else family starve. He start to hit tree with ax, but spirit come back, right out of air again. She say, No cut down tree. I give you better thing. I give you horse. Man think horse very good. He think I take horse back to village. Trade for much food. But he think maybe spirit try to trick him. He say, Let me see horse. Spirit make horse come right out of air, like magic. To man, it look like very good horse. Man very happy, but he not let on. He think he good trader, so maybe he get more. He say, Horse look old. I rather have tree. He get ready to hit tree with ax. Spirit say, Stop! This no ordinary horse. This magic horse. Hit horse with stick three times. You see. Man find stick. Hit side of horse three times. Magic thing happen. Gold coins fall out back side of horse. Man very happy. Try to pick up gold coins, but they gone. Man get angry that spirit trick him. Spirit say, That only to show. You not cut down tree, next time horse make real gold. You keep horse. You keep gold. Man agree. Lead horse away quick before spirit change mind. Man walk on road. He walk and walk, long time. Come to inn. He hungry. He think, I have gold now. Get food. Get drink. Man eat and eat and drink and drink. Time come to pay. Innkeeper say, Give money. Man lead innkeeper outside and tell him stand behind horse. He say, Here is pay. Man hit side of horse three times with stick. But what come out of back side of horse not gold coins. It big smelly pile *phân bón*. *Phân bón* land on innkeeper foot. Innkeeper very angry. He beat man very bad with stick and take horse to pay for food and drink. Man go back to forest to find spirit that trick him. He find place, but tree gone. Only big pile *phân bón* there."

She's told our protagonist a story, a traditional Vietnamese story.

TIP:

The **story within a story** technique is not a common one, but it can be effective. Just make sure you are not dropping it in only for entertainment value; it should, like anything else you put in a story, advance the plot. In this case, it's a way to reveal something about the girl's values.

So, why did I insert the girl's story into my story about a young soldier who is in a foreign bar far from home? The answer is that I'm trying to keep the story from going in the "usual" romance-story direction. That would be boring. The girl's odd behavior of telling a drunken soldier a traditional Vietnamese story, of "communicating" with stories, should catch the reader by surprise, telling them that this second-person story *is not* going to be "predictable."

There is really only one mandatory requirement of a fictional story: it has to be *interesting*. At this point, I'm hoping that the reader will not be able to predict where this story is going and will therefore be *interested* in what is going to happen next.

And what about the content of the girl's story? It contained a message about how greed can lead to disaster. Is it supposed to be a warning to our young soldier, or is it just a way for her to show him how she thinks, what she values?

Earlier, I brought up the subject of reader awareness of writer's intentions. The reader may now be wondering what the writer had in mind by bringing this kind of story in. Is it to characterizes the girl? Or is it a warning about how a person should behave, some kind of foreshadowing?

TIP:

You may wonder where I found the traditional Vietnamese story. Once I decided I wanted the girl to tell him a story, I had to do some research to find the kind of story I was looking for. I wanted an actual traditional Vietnamese story, but it had to be one that would not only characterize the girl, but would also

---

present my protagonist with some kind of message about how a person should *be*.

And that brings up the topic of the role **research** plays in fiction writing. If you are going to insert real-world information into a story, you can be sure some readers will know whether or not the information is accurate.

Accuracy requires research, and if you decide to write a story that requires a lot of research, you'd be well advised to *pick something you'll enjoy researching*.

Let me give you an example. Years ago, I decided I wanted to try out the sub-genre of historical detective/murder mystery fiction. I didn't know much about the American Civil War or the aftermath of it, but I was interested in it, so I decided to create a fictional detective who operated during that troubled period in our nation's history. I had to do a heck of a lot of research about the Civil War and the role it played in the still-evolving history of this nation.

Little did I know what I was getting myself into. I had to read just about everything about the Civil War that's on the internet (there's a lot!), and I also had to buy a whole library of books about it. I now know a lot about both the Civil War and the aftermath, and that research paid off when it led to the writing and publication of my two historical murder-mystery novels, **Who Owns Arizona?** and **The End of the Civil War.**

So, how should we make our protagonist react to the girl's telling of the story? For the moment, I don't think we should have him think too deeply about it. Because he is still in an inebriated state, let's just have him react in a subdued, if a bit confused, way.

> **You open your eyes. It was a funny story, and it makes you feel a little better. She is staring at you. Is she waiting for you to say something?**
> **You say, "Yes, good story. Thank you."**

Our protagonist reacts by thinking it was a funny story. He thanks her (a bit of rare dialogue for him), but he doesn't ask her why she told him that story or what it is supposed to mean. In fact, he doesn't seem to want to think about that at all.

There are times when we want to bring something into a story that will have significance later on, but we want to do it in a way that doesn't necessarily call too much attention to itself. In this case, I want this story event (the girl telling him a traditional Vietnamese story) to be significant enough to be remembered, but for now, I want the reader to pass over it and just continue reading. Next, we have to decide if we want to maintain the pattern of the girl *driving the story.*

TIP:

If you are writing a character-driven story, your protagonist should usually be the one **driving the story** forward. But the concept of driving the action doesn't necessarily mean the protagonist has to be doing all the acting. In this case, the girl is the one acting, and the protagonist is merely reacting. But although the girl is initiating the action, she is not actually driving the story (in terms of reader interest). If the reader is going to keep on turning those pages, it will be because they are interested in what the main character is going to do. Through access to the protagonist's thoughts, the reader is learning how the protagonist sees *the world of the story.* The protagonist is therefore *the center of interest, which is what drives the story forward.*

Now that the girl has finished telling the story, let's keep her in control of the situation.

> **She manages to get you up off the floor and into a chair. She gently explains that the rule is you have to pay money to be with her.**
>
> **She signals to the barman. The barman comes out from behind the bar. You give him money.**
>
> **He goes away.**

The reader may now feel the story is going in a more predictable direction. They may have been expecting the girl to try to get money from our young soldier, and she does. And what will the reader be expecting to happen next? Will she try to get more money from our young soldier? Or does he get more for his money?

If that was all this story was about, it would be a fairly normal romance story.

Let's see if we can continue to surprise the reader.

> **The pretty girl brings your hand up to her cheek. Now your hand is getting wet. Is she crying? Why is she crying?**

Now this should surprise the reader. If the girl really is a prostitute, why would she be crying?

The reader should now know something unusual is going on with this girl. When he first saw the girl, our protagonist thought she looked sad. Here, that sadness is confirmed by her tears (tears are a universal indication of human sadness).

Now let's have the girl act in a way that seems more fitting for this kind of environment.

> **She helps you to your feet, and you put your arm over her shoulders. She's strong, amazingly strong for such a little girl.**
>
> **She helps you stagger down a narrow hallway. You come to a battered wooden door with peeling white paint on it. She opens the door and guides you inside.**

Again, we have the girl leading and our protagonist only following.

Now that the money has been paid, the girl takes our young soldier to a room in the back. I've kept the reader "in the scene" by providing some scene description through his perceptions. He sees, despite his drunken state, a narrow hallway, a battered door, peeling white paint. Once they are inside the room, we can continue to keep him in the observer and reporter role that is typical for these kinds of character-driven stories.

> **You look the room over. It's a small room, this room where the girls bring the boys. Such a grimy little space for doing the so-called love making. A narrow little bed is pushed up against the wall. No other furniture. But why would there need to be anything but a bed in a room like this? For the pretend love making, there is no need for anything but a bed.**

I am not only using protagonist perception to describe the room, I'm also using his thoughts about what he sees as characterization of him.

Next, let's add a bit more richness to the environment of the sad little room, a detail that might reveal more about the culture and the girl.

> **It's dark in the room, except for a bit of flicking light coming from a candle that sits on a cardboard box near the door. A little carved-wood Buddha sits cross-legged behind the candle. The Buddha has a fat tummy. Why do all the carved Buddhas in this country have fat tummies? The people in this country don't have fat tummies. And the little carved Buddha is smiling. Why is he smiling? Is he smiling because he knows what goes on in this room?**

I had him notice the fat tummies of the carved Buddhas, and had him think about the not-so-fat tummies of the Vietnamese people. It continues the process of characterizing him by how he sees the world of the story. The reader will undoubtedly think his take on the smiling Buddha is a bit "odd." They will see that although he is not knowledgeable about the Vietnamese culture, he is curious about it. The reader should begin to think his behavior *and* his perceptions are quite unusual for a young American soldier in this situation.

As I said earlier, in a character-driven story, your protagonist should not only be a good observer of the world of the story, but he should also be the type of person who thinks deeply about what he observes. In this case, I've had him *focus* on something besides the girl.

TIP:

Drawing the reader's attention to something like the carved Buddha is like a **close-up** of an object in a movie (known as an **insert**). It tips the viewers off on something they need to pay attention to.

But that also means writers have to be careful about what they bring the reader's focus to. It may be tempting to describe an interesting object that's in a scene just because it *is* interesting. You have to be aware that readers are always "watching" and are ready to make meaning out of anything you "put" into the story.

Now, let's bring our protagonist's attention back to the girl. What should we have her do next?

Well, given the situation (bar girl takes young soldier boy to a back room), the next step *should be* pretty obvious.

> **The girl leads you to the bed. She helps you take off your clothes.**

As usual, our protagonist reacts (the two-step) with thought.

> **Thank you, nice girl. Better to not have clothes on. Too hot for clothes anyhow.**

Probably just about what the reader would expect. However, what she does next will be less predictable.

> **She pushes you down onto the narrow little bed, and then she stands there looking down at you.**
> **You stare up at her. Why is she looking at you? Does she like to look at your nakedness? But that can't be all she wants. What is going to happen now?**

If I have been successful in getting the reader vicariously involved with the protagonist, the reader will be asking the same thing. At this point, they will probably be convinced that she is just what she seems to be, a prostitute. But let's see if we can continue to make her act in unpredictable ways.

> **She pulls her silken dress over her head and carefully hangs it on a big nail that's been pounded into the wall. She turns to face you.**
>
> **You blink your eyes to clear them. This you want to see clearly.**
>
> **Her slim little naked body is a shimmering marvel in the dim flickering candlelight. It's a beautiful body, more beautiful than you ever imagined a body could be. So thin. So delicate. Her skin looks so smooth and delicious you want to reach out and touch it all over. But for some reason, she won't let you. She is standing back. She doesn't even say anything. She just stands there looking down at you.**

If you want your readers to keep on reading, you have to arouse their curiosity about what is going to happen next. If you have your characters consistently act in predictable ways, their level of curiosity will consistently decrease. Therefore, it's never a bad idea to have characters *seem* to act in predictable ways, and then take a turn toward the unpredictable. Here, I've had the girl take off her clothes —which would be a predictable behavior if she really is a prostitute— but then hold back. That is not likely to have been predicted by the reader. If she really is a prostitute, it seem more likely she would be in a hurry.

So, how should we have our protagonist react to this turn of events? I think we should let him continue to be puzzled and not know how to react.

> **Why doesn't she come to the bed? Isn't that what's supposed to happen? Is she giving you a chance to look at her body before the next part happens?**

The action of the story has stopped as our protagonist (and our reader) waits and wonders what the girl is going to do next. Notice that although little is *happening* in the story, a great deal is going on inside the head of our protagonist. Assuming the reader is now in vicarious involvement with the protagonist, it will still *feel* like the story is moving forward in the sense that the main character in the story is constantly perceiving and reacting.

During this moment of stopped action, we can use the *quiet-moment technique* to give our protagonist time to think through the situation.

TIP:

The **quiet-moment** technique—stopping the story action long enough for the protagonist to think through the situation—is very useful in fiction writing. While the two-step technique gives you a way to show your protagonist's internal response, there are times when you need to have your protagonist think through the overall situation.

It doesn't work very well to have a character thinking complex thoughts in the middle of action or dialogue. Better to create a quiet moment situation during which your protagonist has a bit of time to think things through.

Let's use this quiet-moment of protagonist thinking to give the reader a little more information about him.

> **But wait, you told yourself you didn't want to do the next part. You told yourself you didn't want to be just another sweaty American who pays money to climb on top of one of these little bar girls. You promised yourself your first time should be something special.**

The reader is now aware of some important information about the protagonist: he is a virgin, and he's promised himself he doesn't want his first time to be with a prostitute. That adds character-driven plot to the story: will be stick to his principles and resist this beautiful girl, or is he so smitten by her that he will do anything she wants him to? And what does *she* want him to do?

You might be wondering why I haven't given my protagonist a name. The answer is that I didn't see any need for it. The main reason you need names in a story is so you can notify the reader about who is speaking when you put him into a multi-character conversation. But in this story, I only plan to have two main characters, and I'm thinking the whole story will play out in this back room. Any reference to "him" will therefore refer to the protagonist, and any reference to "her" will refer to the girl who brought him to the room.

In this story, I want the two characters to "represent" something more than named individuals: I want the protagonist to represent a male soldier who might find himself in this kind of situation while serving in a foreign country, and I want the girl to represent a possible female sexual opportunity for that kind of soldier. The story is therefore going to be "about" how this particular young soldier is going to react when confronted by an unusual girl in this kind of situation.

Another reason for not naming the girl is because I want her to be mysterious, almost imaginary, as if he is making her up. Giving her a name could "stabilize" her in the reader's mind and make her less ephemeral. Remember, we've had him think she might not be one of the "usual" girls. Does that mean there is something mysterious about her, or is that just his unreliable perception of her? Let's build on that concept.

> **But maybe this girl is not really one of the usual bar girls. You've never seen her in this place before. And she seems a lot younger than the others. Maybe she's a local girl who just wandered in.**
>
> **But what would a young girl be doing in a place like this if she doesn't work here?**
>
> **No, she has to be one of the bar's girls. She must be new, just in from the countryside. But if she is one of them, why doesn't she come to the bed? Why is she just standing there looking at you?**

We are having our protagonist ask the kind of questions the reader will undoubtedly be asking.

Now, we need to have him make a decision.

> **Okay, if she wants to just look at you, then you should just look at her too. She's really nice to look at. You should take this opportunity to examine every inch of her lovely body.**

From the moment the girl took her clothes off, I kept our protagonist's focus on her body, even as he speculated about what she's up to.

So what's next? It's one of those moments in a story where we could take it in a number of different directions. Now that they are both naked, will he forget about his vow and try to make love to her?

Instead of giving the reader the answer to that question, how about if we put a bit of a twist into the story by diverting his attention away from her body.

> **But then you notice her eyes. Dark eyes. Those eyes are watching you closely. What are those eyes looking for? Are they trying to see inside your brain? Don't bother, pretty girl. Not much in there anymore. Nothing but boozed-out, drugged-out, worn-out mush.**

Here, I've moved his attention away from her body and created another *quiet moment* in which he can think through the situation. As he thinks about what her eyes might be seeing, the reader learns more about how he sees himself.

> **You want to look at her nice body some more, but you can't seem to look away from her eyes. Why is she looking at you like that? And why isn't she in a hurry? The other guys always complain that whenever they go to the back rooms with one of the bar girls, they use their tricks to get you to finish quick, and then they put their pretty white dresses back on right away and go back out to the bar to round up the next guy.**

His thoughts give the reader a bit more information about the bar and about what the girls who work there *usually* do. It adds to the idea that the girl's behavior is unexpected.

By having him focus on the girl's eyes, it gives us the perfect opportunity to have him imagine what she is seeing.

> **Her eyes are calm, but intense, as if they're trying to tell you something. Those dark staring eyes are enough to make a drunk guy not so drunk anymore. What is she seeing? Just another skinny young guy, yet another soldier come from far away to make war on her country, or is she seeing through the pretense, seeing the real you, the lonely, much-less-experienced-with-girls-than-he-pretends-to-be guy who isn't quite sure how the hell he ended up as an American soldier in some God-forsaken hot and steamy country halfway around the world from his home in Arizona? Her eyes may be seeing too much. You have to look away.**

Here, I've had him imagine what the girl is seeing. It's a way to give the reader more information about a protagonist.

TIP:

As I said earlier, one of the problems in telling a story from within the perceptions of a protagonist is that there is no way to describe the protagonist, short of using "**the old mirror trick.**" No one knows us better than we know ourselves, but how do you get self-perception into a story without it seeming contrived. Here is a solution: having your protagonist imagine how another character in the story sees him.

Here, I found a way to provide a little bit of physical description of the him. You might wonder why I haven't provided any physical description of the protagonist before now. The answer is that I didn't see any need for it. And now, describing him simply as "young" and "skinny" is enough to fix his appearance in the reader's mind.

It's now time to restart the story action. Let's put the girl back into action. We can also continue to give our protagonist two-step thought responses as a way to further characterize him.

> **As if your looking away was a signal, she comes to the bed. Is this it? Is it going to happen now? Is what you've been wanting, but resisting, all these years finally going to happen?**
>
> **Maybe you should just let it happen. After all, you're no longer in Arizona, no longer the moody outcast who preferred to spend his time alone in the desert. You said you wanted to change your life. Okay, here's your chance.**

Using character thought, I've given the reader a bit more information about him.

By now, we may have convinced the reader that he is ready to do whatever the girl wants. But what does she want?

> **She lies down next to you.**
> **You hold your breath. What is she going to do?**

The girl is still driving the action, and our protagonist is still wondering what is going to happen next, and assuming our readers are now vicariously involved, they will be wondering the same thing.

TIP:

By giving your readers access to your protagonist's thoughts, you can keep them informed about what your character is **planning** to do.

Sometimes writers will hide their protagonist's thoughts from the reader in order to make story events a surprise. They think that approach builds tension, but it might well do the opposite because it moves readers out of vicarious involvement with the protagonist and puts them into the position of observer. They will end up "watching" and waiting to see what happens instead of *imagining* what is going to happen next.

Readers like to know the **motivations** of a protagonist. Once they "get to know" a character, they like to guess what is going to happen next. If your writing establishes a pattern of keeping them in the dark about the plans of your protagonist, they will soon learn not to bother guessing what is going to happen next. In fact, they may decide not to bother continuing to read your story.

So what should we have the girl do next? They are now in the bed, and they both are naked. Does that mean they are now going to make love?

But what purpose would that serve in a story about a confused young soldier's encounter with a mysterious girl? We have to be careful not to paint ourselves into a mundane ending. After all, this example story is supposed to be a demonstration of how to use second-person to indicate a protagonist with psychological issues. Therefore, we need to start moving the story more in that direction.

> **But she doesn't do anything. She just lies there, staring at you. As you try to push away the remaining cobwebs of drugs and alcohol, you wonder what you are supposed to do now. Are you supposed to grab her and begin? She's probably waiting for you to begin. You're feeling a bit shy. But why should you feel shy? She's the girl. You're the guy. She's the one at risk, completely naked, in bed with a foreign soldier who is also naked. She's entirely vulnerable. In fact, she's so young and so thin, she looks fragile. Not only that, but in her country, what she's doing is undoubtedly considered to be shameful.**

The reader, ready to see what he is going to do, may now be forced to consider the possibility that he isn't going to do anything. As the story goes along, that odd passivity can become more and more relevant to the plot.

The paragraph also brings a cross-cultural issue into the story. He believes what she is doing would be considered shameful in her country. Whether he has evidence for that or if is just his speculation doesn't matter; it is his belief, and therefore, it affects his *motivation*. It justifies his unwillingness to act.

TIP:

You should not skimp on providing the reader with plenty of information about a character's **motives**. Nothing can "push" a reader out of a story faster than a protagonist who acts in a way the reader feels is unlikely. That means the groundwork about a character's motivation needs to be laid *before* the character acts.

To reinforce the idea that our protagonist is psychologically unable to act, let's have him think a bit more about his own motives.

> **But her eyes are not ashamed, and that makes *you* feel ashamed. You tell yourself you should stop your damn foolish lusting after this fragile young girl long enough to ask yourself just what the hell you think you're doing.**
>
> **Well, you know very well what you intended to do. You were intending to do what all the other soldiers do to these girls in these back rooms.**
>
> **Well, it's what you're supposed to do, isn't it? Isn't it what these girls are paid to let you do to them? So, why aren't you doing it? You should have gone ahead and done it the moment she took off her dress. Even though you've never done it before, you know how to do it, so why hesitate now?**
>
> **But still, you are unsure. Why? Is it because those dark eyes are watching you? Those eyes. So calm. So intense.**

At this point, I've put our protagonist on the fence. Will he or won't he? He is thinking he should have gone ahead and made love to the girl, but something about her eyes has stopped him.

The girl is not acting as the protagonist (and the reader) would expect her to act, and that creates a "why" plot. To keep the character-driven plot going (and hold off the resolution for a bit longer), let's have our protagonist again try to think through the situation.

> **You have to think. You turn onto your back and look up at the ceiling. Parts of it are peeling away and hanging down like thick cobwebs. It reminds you of where you are; you are in a grimy little room in the back of a sleazy bar and whorehouse in Saigon.**

This paragraph provides a little more description of the room, which helps to "keep the reader in the scene." It also creates another *quiet moment* pause in the action so the protagonist can think through the situation.

> **Well, so what? You tell yourself to snap out of it and enjoy this. You paid good money to be in this room with this girl. Shouldn't you at least enjoy looking at her body?**
>
> **You turn back to face her. You let your eyes wander over her entire naked body. She's beautiful. Just beautiful.**
>
> **You try to find another word to describe her. She's . . . flawless. Yes, that's the word, flawless. She's perfect, as if no man has ever touched her before this moment.**
>
> **But is that possible? Such perfection hardly seems possible here in this dingy little back room. She isn't acting like the other bar girls, but if she isn't one of them, what is she doing here? Was she forced into this? You imagine somebody threatening her, Maybe they are holding her family hostage unless she does this. Or maybe it's her parents who are making her do this. They need money, and she's a good girl, loyal to them, wanting to help them, no matter what she has to do.**

Here, I'm walking a fine line. As I said earlier, readers *do* tend to believe protagonist speculation, but in this case, I'm having him grasp at straws. It's another example of the *unreliable narrator* technique. I don't really want the reader to think the girl is being forced to do what she's doing, so I'm having him think through some scenarios that are unlikely. I'm expecting readers to agree that there *is* something wrong with this situation, but I don't want them to necessarily go along with the conclusions he's coming up with. To make sure the reader "gets it" that his thoughts are only speculation, let's have him doubt his own ideas.

> **But would they send such a young girl into a place like this? She's little more than a child.**
>
> **And that thought startles you. Just how young is this girl? In the flickering light of the candles, it's hard to be sure, but she looks pretty damn young. You sit up to look at her more closely. There's no doubt about it, she is young, very young. She's very thin, and her breasts are too undeveloped to really be considered a woman, even in this insane country where lots of child-women earn American dollars by selling their bodies.**
>
> **A word creeps into your mind: forbidden. This is a child. Back home, they would call her "jail-bait." Back in America you could be put in prison for what you're thinking about doing to this young girl.**
>
> **She waits, still calmly watching you, allowing you to look at her body all you want.**
>
> **The situation is very confusing. You begin to doubt this is even real. That last joint you smoked must have been a lot more potent than you thought. Or maybe they put something in that last drink that put you into a dream.**

In this segment, I'm again using the unreliable narrator technique. I'm having the protagonist begin to think this strange situation is unreal, perhaps a dream. I don't want our readers to think the scene *is* a dream, but I do want them to think that from the protagonist's POV it is "dream like." As we go forward, I want the story to gradually seem more dream like, but I want the reader to "see" clearly what is going on. Let's see if we can maintain that delicate balance.

> But it feels real. You can feel the warm moist air of the room. You can feel the damp pressure of your own naked body against the mattress. Yes, it all seems completely real. And she seems real too, more real and more wonderful than anything that's ever happened to you in your entire life.
>
> Okay, this must not be a dream. She's just waiting, waiting for you to start. But if that's it, why isn't she in a hurry? If she's here to provide sex for money, why isn't she urging you to do it and get it over with?
>
> But she doesn't seem to be in a hurry, and she hasn't uttered a word since the two of you entered this room.
>
> You have to decide what to do before it's too late. There's probably a time limit for this. When your time is up, someone will probably come in and make you leave.

I've had the protagonist think through the situation in yet another *quiet moment*. Now, the reader will probably be ready for him to take some action. But will he?

> Finally, she reaches out to pull you close.
>
> So this is it. It's about to finally happen. Your whole body is ready for it. You feel her firm little breasts against your chest. You wait.
>
> But she doesn't do anything else.
>
> She must be waiting for you to do something. You cautiously put your arm between your two bodies. She doesn't react. You slowly begin to move your hand down toward that thin triangle of girlish hair you saw between her legs. You move your hand very slowly, almost apologetically, but just as the tips of your fingers cautiously begin to touch the first few delicate hairs, she gently moves your hand away and whispers, "Shh, shh."

He finally acts, and she reacts to stop him, using a tiny bit of dialogue. Up to now, the scene has been playing out without dialogue. In order to get the reader to focus on character action and interior thought, I've mostly held off using *the dialogue tool*.

TIP:

Dialogue is a normal part of almost all modern fiction, but it should be applied consciously as a tool that serves a specific purpose.

At various points in a story, you may have to decide whether to use narration, action, character thought, or dialogue. If you choose dialogue, you should always remember that dialogue *characterizes* the speaker.

The girl utters a phrase that seems to be intended to slow him down. Is she unwilling to have sex with him, or does she just want to remain in control? The reader should, by now, be asking the same question.

Let's have our protagonist ask himself those kinds of questions.

What does shh mean? Does it mean she really *doesn't* want you to make love to her? Maybe it's her way of telling you she's too young.

Yes, it's true. She *is* too young. For that reason, you should be content to just lie here next to her.

But do you feel content? It's strange, but you *do*. The feeling of agitated worry that's normally lurking inside you seems to be slipping away. Maybe you're even feeling a little bit happy. Can that be? Happy? It's like remembering an old feeling that you haven't known for a long time. You might even be feeling so comfortable you're getting sleepy.

But no, you don't want to go to sleep! You don't want to let this moment go. If you don't hold her tight, she might disappear into the night and go back to whatever dream she came from.

In response to her moving his hand away, he immediately stops trying to touch her. It shows his passivity and the affect she is having on him. He rationalizes his going along with her wishes by telling himself that she's too young to make love to, that just being in bed with such beautiful young girl should be enough.

Actually, we've solved his problem to some degree. Even though he is attracted to this young girl, he didn't really want his first sexual experience to be with a prostitute. She is giving him an excuse to continue not acting, an excuse for not doing the usual male thing and taking the lead.

Here again, we need to look at the issue of motivation. From the beginning, I've developed my protagonist as a passive person. He is not reacting the way a soldier normally would, and he knows it. He doesn't think about what that says about him as a soldier, but that has been part of the subtext of this story all along.

Now it's time to bring that issue to the forefront.

TIP:

Most writers are aware of the concept of **subtext**, but using it effectively in a story is not so easy. Subtext lies in undertone, something the writer does not want explicitly stated. Not so easy to pull off. If we intend for something to be part of the story, but we don't overtly put it into the story, how can we be sure the reader is going to "get it"?

In this case, the reader may have temporarily forgotten that our young protagonist is a draftee who is not acting with the kind of forthrightness that soldier-training is supposed to lead to. I want the subtextual issue of how young soldiers are supposed to act in a time of war to be an important part of the story. In my *Vietnam War* novel, that issue starts out as subtext, but eventually becomes a primary focus in the story.

Now, let's give the girl some dialogue, which may (or may not) reveal why she brought the young soldier to this back room.

We can also give our protagonist some dialogue to have him try to explain himself to her.

You're still trying to fight off your sleepy feeling
when she puts her lips close to your ear and whispers,
"You no should be here. You wrong for this place."

That wakes you up. Shouldn't be here? Be where?
In this room? In this country? What does she mean?

"Much danger for you here." Her voice is urgent.

Danger? That's for sure. Isn't there a war going on
in this country? But maybe that's not what she meant.
Maybe she somehow understands that you didn't want
to be here, didn't want to be a soldier. You should
explain it to her. "Back home . . . in my country, when
you get to a certain age, you get drafted. Into the
Army, you know? You don't have a choice. They make
you—"

She puts her finger to your lips. "No talk," she
whispers. "You listen. I tell story."

Another story? Will it be another old Vietnamese
story, like the first one? That would be good. You like
her stories.

She whispers into your ear:

"Man catch soft-shell turtle. Bring turtle home to
eat. Tell servant girl kill turtle. Cook turtle for supper.
Man go away. Servant girl get out knife. Start water
boil. But turtle talk. Say, Please no kill. I hurt no one.
Eat no flesh. Eat only green plant next to river.
Please let go. Someday you get reward. Girl have
knife in hand. Girl not know what to do. Master say
want eat turtle for supper. Turtle say, Please. Take
to river. Servant girl look at knife in hand. Throw
down knife. Hide turtle in sack. Take to river. Let turtle go into water. When master find out, he very
angry. He tell girl go away from house. Never return.
Poor servant girl thrown out on street. Only clothes
on back. Man tell neighbors not hire girl. Girl have
no place to go. Cold rain come. She go to river to
hide under wooden bridge. Girl have no food to eat.
No blanket. She get very cold. She get very weak.
She get sick and have terrible fever. She sure she
going to die. Turtle come up out of water. See girl

> under bridge. Turtle cover girl with mud. Special mud from bottom of river. Make girl warm. Turtle bring girl fine green water plant and good white water root to eat. Girl feel better. People see turtle help girl by river. Bring other people to see. It miracle, they say. Master of girl come. He see miracle too. He say he sorry. He take girl back to house and let her be like daughter. He tell people he never eat turtle again."

Here, I've brought in another traditional Vietnamese story. The first story was interesting and funny, but this second story, about being in the role of killer versus being the type of person who spares lives, seems much more serious because it comes immediately after her telling him that he is in danger. What will our protagonist think of this new story? Let's have him struggle to figure it out.

> **She is staring into your eyes. What is that look? A question? Is she asking if you understood the story? Did you? It was a story about being kind to animals. Okay, it was a nice story, but why did she tell you *that* story? Did it have something to do with that thing she said about you being in danger?**
>
> **You try to think of something to say, anything to make her happy. "Nice story," you say. "Poor little servant girl. She got thrown out, and then she got sick. Not fair. All she did was save a—"**
>
> **Again, she puts her delicate little finger to your lips. "You listen." Her eyes are urgent. "Time come, they say kill. You must not kill."**
>
> **What a strange thing to say. Does it mean you're supposed to be like the servant girl and not kill poor little animals? Nothing wrong with that idea. Being kind to animals is probably part of their Buddhist tradition. But wait, what if she's not talking about killing things like turtles? What if she's talking about killing people? Like maybe killing some of her Vietnamese people?**

The girl's warning and her second story has completely changed the mood. It catches our protagonist off guard, and it probably will do the same thing to the reader. How is he going to respond? Let's have him respond with confusion.

> **You stare into her dark eyes to try to figure out what her story meant. But those eyes have no answers.**
> **So dark, so intense, those eyes. What do those eyes want from you? A promise? But doesn't she know you're a soldier? Soldiers are supposed to kill the enemy when they are told to, and the enemy *is* people, even though they say a good soldier isn't supposed to think about that.**

There are times in a story when you might have to leave the reader wondering. This is one of those times. In today's character-driven stories, a writer's main goal is to get the reader vicariously involved with the protagonist. You don't want your reader to be passively "watching" the story play out, as if they were watching some mindless sitcom on TV that even tells you when to laugh. You want them to think about what they would do in such a situation.

So, if we are going to end this story with the reader still vicariously involved, we need to create a *denouement* that maintains the character-driven plot.

TIP:
Denouement is a term from the French that refers to the final scenes of a story. It resolves all the story issues and ties up all the loose ends to bring the story to a close.

In this story, the plot relates to personal issues the protagonist is struggling with. Therefore, the conclusion of the story should relate to the resolution of those issues.

Earlier, I talked about *character arc*, the concept that a character should have changed, and maybe grown, as a result of experiencing the story's events. So, how has this night's encounter with a strange Vietnamese girl changed our protagonist?

To show that, let's have our protagonist struggle to think it through.

> **You want to ask her questions about what she meant, but before you can speak, she lies back down next to you and says, "No talk now. You sleep."**
> **She wants you to sleep. But you don't want to sleep. You don't want this night with this beautiful girl to end with sleep.**

Here, I'm using character thought to foreshadow. The girl has been in charge of the situation throughout. Is she now trying to get him to sleep so she can slip away? Let's stick with our protagonist's thoughts to show his response to her power of suggestion.

> **You don't want to go to sleep, but your eyelids are feeling very heavy. Maybe you should close your eyes, just for a few minutes.**

I think the reader will "get" that he is going to fall asleep. Now we need to show what happens when he wakes up.

> **You open your eyes. It is still dark.**
> **Something is wrong, very wrong. Your sleepy peacefulness is gone, and you are sweating. Why are you sweating? Are you afraid? Why are you afraid?**

I'm again using the self-questioning technique to take the reader into our protagonist's thoughts. As I said earlier, self-questioning can be an effective way to show protagonist emotions like anxiety or fear or confusion. Now, let's have him remember where he is and try to think through what happened.

> **Then you remember, you are in Vietnam, a very long way from home. You were in a bar. You took drugs. There was booze. You drank too much booze. You ended up under a table.**

I'm using short declarative sentences to indicate a mind struggling to piece reality back together. By having him think through the sequence of events that took place, I'm reminding the reader of what has happened so far in the story.

> **You were brought to a back room with . . . Wait! There was a girl, a beautiful young girl! Is she still here? You reach out into the darkness, but your hands find nothing but the wadded-up pillow. The sweat-stained pillow is trying to deny that she was ever here. It's trying to tell you she wasn't real, that you dreamed her. Can that be? But everything seems so real, the night, the room, the noises coming from the street outside: shrill voices arguing, a dog barking in the distance, a motorbike passing with harsh overconfident loudness. So she had to be real too, didn't she? She told you stories. She was naked. So slim. So enticing. Wasn't she in this very bed, right here next to you?**

Again, the self questioning technique in second-person shows his confusion and self doubt. Let's continue that approach and also remind the reader of where he is.

> **But if she really was here, why did she go away? The room seems sad and empty and dark without her. Wasn't there flickering candlelight? And a little carved Buddha? She took the candlelight and the Buddha away with her, so now there's nothing left but the darkness and the emptiness.**

I'm having his confused thoughts about where he is and what happened in the night morph into self-analysis of his physical condition, and then I transition into self-questioning thoughts about why he feels so bad.

This is crucial moment in the story: will he snap out of it, or will he sink further into confusion and doubt? He seems to be on a knife edge, struggling to hold onto reality, but in danger of losing the thread of it. Why? What was it about the girl and the strange night in the bar's back room that's thrown him so off balance? He has to try to think it through. But where will that lead him? Into more confusion, or somewhere worse?

> **You try to sit up, but you can't do it. You just don't have the strength. You lie back, out of breath. You stare up into the darkness. You have to try to think this through. You're in Saigon, Vietnam, a strange and fearsome foreign country. But *why* are you here? You have to put the pieces of the puzzle together. Use your brain. Think. Okay, you are in the Army. You got sent to this place, a place you shouldn't be.**
>
> **But wait! Didn't *she* say that? Yes! *She* said you shouldn't be here. Somehow she knew you don't belong here. But how did she know? How could she know how wrong and pointless it all is? The war. Pointless. Us Americans being here. Wrong. You pretending to be a soldier. Wrong *and* pointless.**

Here, the heavy use of "you" by the protagonist to refer to himself shows the power of second-person to show the workings of a troubled mind.

As we saw in the first-person example story in the previous chapter, character-driven plot arises out of a protagonist trying to solve a personal dilemma or challenge. Now the reader can see our young protagonist's personal challenge: how is he going to break out of his endless cycle of depression and drug dependency.

As I said before, one of the keys to a successful ending of any character-driven story is to show character arc. But writers should be aware that character arc does not necessarily mean *growth*; in fiction, the term only refers to a change in the protagonist that takes place due to what happened in the story. What keeps the sense of plot alive (in the reader's mind) is that he *may not* find new solutions to his dilemma; in fact, he may end up in a worse place than where he started.

So, which way is our protagonist going to go after the experience of a night in a bar's back room with a beautiful, but very young, girl?

Let's use the self-questioning approach to have him try to find some answers to that question.

> **But if you aren't a soldier, what are you? Well, she showed you what you are, a make-believe soldier in a make-believe war. How could you not have seen it before?**

Here, he is beginning to lose his grip on reality. Being with the girl made him feel more at peace with himself, but awaking without her has resulted in a rebound effect, leaving him in even worse shape than he was before.

Let's have him think back to how he got himself into this situation.

> **The whole idea of being a soldier was a mistake, and somehow she knew it. The stupid idea overtook you that night you were sleeping on the ground out in the Arizona desert after yet another one of your long solitary hikes. It came to you in the middle of the night as you stared up at the infinite array of stars. You were shivering from the cold, and the moody desert sounds were talking to you about your wasted life, your pointless existence, your reliance on drugs and alcohol to make meaning out of it all. Those night sounds convinced you that you should do something worthwhile, like maybe you should join the Army. You were going to get drafted pretty soon anyhow, so why not go fight the Communist off there in that Vietnam place they are always showing on the TV.**
>
> **The next morning, the cold clear reality of pragmatic cactus plants and restless coyotes tracks all around your campsite made the idea seem real, even logical. At least your life would have a purpose.**
>
> **So you volunteered for the draft. You went through Army training, and before you even had a chance to think about what you'd done, they sent you here.**
>
> **And for a while, it worked. You had a new purpose in life. You were in a strange, but interesting, new country. There was a war, but you were in no real danger. All you had to do was work in the supply warehouse all day and then go out drinking every night.**

Here, I'm using protagonist thought and memory to provide the reader with significant backstory to show how, and why, he ended up as a soldier in Vietnam.

TIP:

If you decide **backstory** information is necessary before the reader can fully understand the character, then you have to decide where to insert it into the story. *Usually, backstory is inserted near the start.* But in this case I wanted to create a feeling of *immediacy* at the start of the story. Therefore, I decided to hold off inserting much backstory until his mental problems became the front and center issue.

Notice that I used *memory* of his night in the desert rather than a fully-developed *flashback* scene.

Now that the reader has the backstory of how our protagonist ended up playing the role of a soldier in Vietnam, we can end this story by showing his thoughts as he searches for, and eventually finds, a solution to his personal dilemma.

But then a strange girl got inside your mind and took everything away. She left you empty. Empty of purpose. Empty of expectations. Anything you had, or thought you had, before is gone. Your dream of being a heroic soldier going off to fight in a glorious foreign war has been revealed for what it was, a naive self-delusion, a childish fantasy. You are nothing but what you have always been, directionless, confused, unsure of yourself, often depressed, and now stuck for at least a year in Vietnam, the last place one earth you should be.

But there is one thing she can't take away from you —the solution. All you have to do is admit that your stupid life is just going to get worse and worse, so you can finally give up your ridiculous hopes and fantasies and pour enough strong Vietnamese booze into your body and inhale enough strong Vietnamese pot smoke

> **into your lungs to finally convince your brain that you are serious about not wanting to do this stupid reality anymore so it will finally oblige by shutting the whole damn thing down to the extent that you can once again be absolutely sure that nothing matters at all, not even a strange Vietnamese girl who might not have even been real anyhow.**

I ended this second-person, character-driven story of a troubled young soldier by showing him unable to deal with his life without the aid of alcohol and drugs.

Although some readers may be sorry to see such a disappointing ending, I believe it is the most realistic outcome.

In this second-person, unreliable narrator story, we've led our mentally fragile protagonist into a dream-like encounter with a strange girl. Clearly, he was not prepared to deal with the situation. While most young soldiers in a foreign land would be eager to find themselves in a sexual situation with a young local girl, this particular soldier approaches the encounter passively, letting the girl take all the leads. As the scene develops, it becomes clear that the young soldier is not looking for sex; he is searching for a solution to his personal problems. As the encounter evolves, he starts to believe the girl can provide him with answers. She gives him hope. He begins to believe he might be able to live a better, more peaceful, life as long as he has her.

But in the end, she disappears and he feels abandoned. It leaves him even sadder and more troubled than before, proving to him once and for all that his former solution, drugs and alcohol is the *only* solution.

I *could have* created a somewhat more hopeful ending by suggesting that the encounter with the girl told him that he needed to find professional help. But would it be realistic to suggest that such help was available for the nearly three million young soldiers who served in the Vietnam War?

Review

Below is a reprint of the completed story. As you review the story, look for the fiction-writing techniques we explored in this chapter, including:

- Developing a scene which conveys the most **important elements of the locale** (the **environment** in which the majority of the story events will take place).
- Introducing the reader to the world of the story through **protagonist perception** to create **vicarious involvement** with the protagonist.
- Creating a **"feel" of protagonist self-doubt and estrangement** from the self through the use of **second-person pronouns**.
- Getting the reader vicarious involved with the protagonist through the use of the action/reaction **two-step**.
- **Characterizing the protagonist** by showing how he "sees" the world of the story.
- Relaying information about **the situation** through **protagonist thought**.
- Establishing the protagonist's storytelling "**voice**."
- Creating an **unreliable narrator** by showing the reader that the protagonist's perceptions are not always accurate.
- Using the **story-within-a-story** technique to create **subtext**.
- Creating **romantic interest** through protagonist perception.
- Sticking to **one point of view** unless you have a **good reason** to do otherwise.
- Letting the **events of the story** play out in a **linear** fashion.
- Keeping the reader **in the scene**.
- Using **sentence fragments** to convey the "feel" of **character thought**.
- Using the **self-questioning technique** to convey the "feel" of character **doubt and confusion**.

- Using the **quiet-moment technique** to give the protagonist time to **think through** the situation.
- Using **memory** rather than **flashback** to provide the reader with **backstory** information.

Saigon Fable

Back in Basic Training, they said if you get sent to a foreign country like Vietnam you should behave in a way that upholds the honor of the U.S. Army. One thing for sure, lying drunk on a dirty barroom floor in Saigon, staring up at the underside of a table, is not behaving in a way that upholds the honor of the U.S. Army.

You are hearing noise. Loud music. Loud voices. Drunken men shouting, drunken men fighting, drunken men not upholding the honor of the U.S. Army.

A face appears. The face is looking at you. Your blurry eyes try to focus. It's a Vietnamese face. A pretty Vietnamese girl face.

"Hello, pretty girl face."

Did you say that out loud?

The pretty girl face is coming closer. Is she one of the usual girls? If only you could make your eyes focus, you might recognize her. Maybe she's a new girl. If only you could make your tongue talk, you could ask her why she looks so sad.

She sits down on the floor next to you.

Sure, sit right down here, pretty girl. You can share my floor.

She takes your hand. Her hand is small. It's a delicate hand, a caring hand, a hand that wants you to be happy, to be at peace, to not be so worried all the time.

Who is this girl? Even with your blurry eyes, you can tell she's more beautiful than any girl you have seen in the entire twenty years of your wasted life. She's thin, exotic, almost dream-like in her white silk dress.

Still holding your hand, she leans close.

You feel the lightest brush of her hair against your cheek. You close your eyes. You detect the scent of . . . flowers? No, something else. But what?

She is whispering in your ear. With the chaos of the bar all around the two of you—men drinking, men gambling, men shouting, men fighting, men not upholding the honor of the US Army—she seems to be telling you some kind of story:

"Long time ago, poor man go to forest. Family starve. He want find wood. Want trade wood for food. But when he get to forest place, wood all gone. Trees all cut down. He walk and walk, but see no tree. Then he see one tree all alone. It look like very good tree. Man very happy. He think, I cut down tree. Take back to village. Get food for family. Man get ready to hit tree with ax, but very beautiful woman come right out of air. She stand in front of tree. She say, Stop! No cut down tree. I spirit of forest. I live in tree. Last tree left in forest. She disappear. Strange smell left behind, like flower, sweet flower man never smell before. Man drop ax and rub eyes. Did he really see spirit? Maybe he imagine her. He not want to make spirit of forest mad, but he need tree. Else family starve. He start to hit tree with ax, but spirit come back, right out of air again. She say, No cut down tree. I give you better thing. I give you horse. Man think horse very good. He think I take horse back to village. Trade for much food. But he think maybe spirit try to trick him. He say, Let me see horse. Spirit make horse come right out of air, like magic. To man, it look like very good horse. Man very happy, but he not let on. He think he good trader, so maybe he get more. He say, Horse look old. I rather have tree. He get ready to hit tree with ax. Spirit say, Stop! This no ordinary horse. This magic horse. Hit horse with stick three times. You see. Man find stick. Hit side of horse three times. Magic thing happen. Gold coins fall out back side of horse. Man very happy. Try to pick up gold coins, but they gone. Man get angry that spirit trick him. Spirit say, That only to show. You not cut down tree, next time horse make real gold. You keep horse. You keep gold. Man agree. Lead horse away quick before spirit change mind. Man walk on road. He walk and walk, long time. Come to inn. He hungry. He think, I have gold now. Get food. Get drink. Man eat and eat and drink and drink. Time come to pay. Innkeeper say, Give money. Man lead innkeeper outside and tell him stand behind horse. He say, Here is pay. Man hit side of horse three times with stick. But what come out of back side of horse not gold coins. It big smelly pile *phân bón*. *Phân bón* land on innkeeper foot. Innkeeper very angry. He beat man very bad with stick and take horse to pay for food and drink. Man go back to forest to find spirit that trick him. He find place, but tree gone. Only big pile *phân bón* there."

You open your eyes. It was a funny story, and it makes you feel a little better. She is staring at you. Is she waiting for you to say something?

You say, "Yes, good story. Thank you."

She manages to get you up off the floor and into a chair. She gently explains that the rule is you have to pay money to be with her.

She signals to the barman. The barman comes out from behind the bar. You give him money.

He goes away.

The pretty girl brings your hand up to her cheek. Now your hand is getting wet. Is she crying? Why is she crying?

She helps you to your feet, and you put your arm over her shoulders. She's strong, amazingly strong for such a little girl.

She helps you stagger down a narrow hallway. You come to a battered wooden door with peeling white paint on it. She opens the door and guides you inside.

You look the room over. It's a small room, this room where the girls bring the boys. Such a grimy little space for doing the so-called love making. A narrow little bed is pushed up against the wall. No other furniture. But why would there need to be anything but a bed in a room like this? For the pretend love making, there is no need for anything but a bed.

It's dark in the room, except for a bit of flicking light coming from a candle that sits on a cardboard box near the door. A little carved-wood Buddha sits cross-legged behind the candle. The

Buddha has a fat tummy. Why do all the carved Buddhas in this country have fat tummies? The people in this country don't have fat tummies. And the little carved Buddha is smiling. Why is he smiling? Is he smiling because he knows what goes on in this room?

The girl leads you to the bed. She helps you take off your clothes.

Thank you, nice girl. Better to not have clothes on. Too hot for clothes anyhow.

She pushes you down onto the narrow little bed, and then she stands there looking down at you.

You stare up at her. Why is she looking at you? Does she like to look at your nakedness? But that can't be all she wants. What is going to happen now?

She pulls her silken dress over her head and carefully hangs it on a big nail that's been pounded into the wall. She turns to face you.

You blink your eyes to clear them. This you want to see clearly.

Her slim little naked body is a shimmering marvel in the dim flickering candlelight. It's a beautiful body, more beautiful than you ever imagined a body could be. So thin. So delicate. Her skin looks so smooth and delicious you want to reach out and touch it all over. But for some reason, she won't let you. She is standing back. She doesn't even say anything. She just stands there looking down at you.

Why doesn't she come to the bed? Isn't that what's supposed to happen? Is she giving you a chance to look at her body before the next part happens?

But wait, you told yourself you didn't want to do the next part. You told yourself you didn't want to be just another sweaty American who pays money to climb on top of one of these little bar girls. You promised yourself your first time should be something special.

But maybe this girl is not really one of the usual bar girls. You've never seen her in this place before. And she seems a lot younger than the others. Maybe she's a local girl who just wandered in.

But what would a young girl be doing in a place like this if she doesn't work here?

No, she has to be one of the bar's girls. She must be new, just in from the countryside. But if she is one of them, why doesn't she come to the bed? Why is she just standing there looking at you?

Okay, if she wants to just look at you, then you should just look at her too. She's really nice to look at. You should take this opportunity to examine every inch of her lovely body.

But then you notice her eyes. Dark eyes. Those eyes are watching you closely. What are those eyes looking for? Are they trying to see inside your brain? Don't bother, pretty girl. Not much in there anymore. Nothing but boozed-out, drugged-out, worn-out mush.

You want to look at her nice body some more, but you can't seem to look away from her eyes. Why is she looking at you like that? And why isn't she in a hurry? The other guys always complain that whenever they go to the back rooms with one of the bar girls, they use their tricks to get you to finish quick, and then they put their pretty white dresses back on right away and go back out to the bar to round up the next guy.

Her eyes are calm, but intense, as if they're trying to tell you something. Those dark staring eyes are enough to make a drunk guy not so drunk anymore. What is she seeing? Just another skinny young guy, yet another soldier come from far away to make war on her country, or is she seeing through the pretense, seeing the real you, the lonely, much-less-experienced-with-girls-than-he-pretends-to-be guy who isn't quite sure how the hell he ended up as an American soldier in some God-forsaken hot and steamy country halfway around the world from his home in Arizona? Her eyes may be seeing too much. You have to look away.

As if your looking away was a signal, she comes to the bed. Is this it? Is it going to happen now? Is what you've been wanting, but resisting, all these years finally going to happen?

Maybe you should just let it happen. After all, you're no longer in Arizona, no longer the moody outcast who preferred to spend his time alone in the desert. You said you wanted to change your life. Okay, here's your chance.

She lies down next to you.

You hold your breath. What is she going to do?

But she doesn't do anything. She just lies there, staring at you. As you try to push away the remaining cobwebs of drugs and alcohol, you wonder what you are supposed to do now. Are you supposed to grab her and begin? She's probably waiting for you to begin. You're feeling a bit shy. But why should you feel shy? She's the girl. You're the guy. She's the one at risk, completely naked, in bed with a foreign soldier who is also naked. She's entirely vulnerable. In fact, she's so young and so thin, she looks fragile. Not only that, but in her country, what she's doing is undoubtedly considered to be shameful.

But her eyes are not ashamed, and that makes *you* feel ashamed. You tell yourself you should stop your damn foolish lusting after this fragile young girl long enough to ask yourself just what the hell you think you're doing.

Well, you know very well what you intended to do. You were intending to do what all the other soldiers do to these girls in these back rooms.

Well, it's what you're supposed to do, isn't it? Isn't it what these girls are paid to let you do to them? So, why aren't you doing it? You should have gone ahead and done it the moment she took off her dress. Even though you've never done it before, you know how to do it, so why hesitate now?

But still, you are unsure. Why? Is it because those dark eyes are watching you? Those eyes. So calm. So intense.

You have to think. You turn onto your back and look up at the ceiling. Parts of it are peeling away and hanging down like thick cobwebs. It reminds you of where you are; you are in a grimy little room in the back of a sleazy bar and whorehouse in Saigon.

Well, so what? You tell yourself to snap out of it and enjoy this. You paid good money to be in this room with this girl. Shouldn't you at least enjoy looking at her body?

You turn back to face her. You let your eyes wander over her entire naked body. She's beautiful. Just beautiful.

You try to find another word to describe her. She's . . . flawless. Yes, that's the word, flawless. She's perfect, as if no man has ever touched her before this moment.

But is that possible? Such perfection hardly seems possible here in this dingy little back room. She isn't acting like the other bar girls, but if she isn't one of them, what is she doing here? Was she forced into this? You imagine somebody threatening her, Maybe they are holding her family hostage unless she does this. Or maybe it's her parents who are making her do this. They need money, and she's a good girl, loyal to them, wanting to help them, no matter what she has to do.

But would they send such a young girl into a place like this? She's little more than a child.

And that thought startles you. Just how young is this girl? In the flickering light of the candles, it's hard to be sure, but she looks pretty damn young. You sit up to look at her more closely. There's no doubt about it, she is young, very young. She's very thin, and her breasts are too undeveloped to really be considered a woman, even in this insane country where lots of child-women earn American dollars by selling their bodies.

A word creeps into your mind: forbidden. This is a child. Back home, they would call her "jail-bait." Back in America you could be put in prison for what you're thinking about doing to this young girl.

She waits, still calmly watching you, allowing you to look at her body all you want.

The situation is very confusing. You begin to doubt this is even real. That last joint you smoked must have been a lot more potent than you thought. Or maybe they put something in that last drink that put you into a dream.

But it feels real. You can feel the warm moist air of the room. You can feel the damp pressure of your own naked body against the mattress. Yes, it all seems completely real. And she seems real too, more real and more wonderful than anything that's ever happened to you in your entire life.

Okay, this must not be a dream. She's just waiting, waiting for you to start. But if that's it, why isn't she in a hurry? If she's here to provide sex for money, why isn't she urging you to do it and get it over with?

But she doesn't seem to be in a hurry, and she hasn't uttered a word since the two of you entered this room.

You have to decide what to do before it's too late. There's probably a time limit for this. When your time is up, someone will probably come in and make you leave.

Finally, she reaches out to pull you close.

So this is it. It's about to finally happen. Your whole body is ready for it. You feel her firm little breasts against your chest. You wait.

But she doesn't do anything else.

She must be waiting for you to do something. You cautiously put your arm between your two bodies. She doesn't react. You slowly begin to move your hand down toward that thin triangle of girlish hair you saw between her legs. You move your hand very slowly, almost apologetically, but just as the tips of your fingers cautiously begin to touch the first few delicate hairs, she gently moves your hand away and whispers, "Shh, shh."

What does shh mean? Does it mean she really *doesn't* want you to make love to her? Maybe it's her way of telling you she's too young.

Yes, it's true. She *is* too young. For that reason, you should be content to just lie here next to her.

But do you feel content? It's strange, but you *do*. The feeling of agitated worry that's normally lurking inside you seems to be slipping away. Maybe you're even feeling a little bit happy. Can that be? Happy? It's like remembering an old feeling that you haven't known for a long time. You might even be feeling so comfortable you're getting sleepy.

But no, you don't want to go to sleep! You don't want to let this moment go. If you don't hold her tight, she might disappear into the night and go back to whatever dream she came from.

You're still trying to fight off your sleepy feeling when she puts her lips close to your ear and whispers, "You no should be here. You wrong for this place."

That wakes you up. Shouldn't be here? Be where? In this room? In this country? What does she mean?

"Much danger for you here." Her voice is urgent.

Danger? That's for sure. Isn't there a war going on in this country? But maybe that's not what she meant. Maybe she somehow understands that you didn't want to be here, didn't want to be a soldier. You should explain it to her. "Back home . . . in my country, when you get to a certain age, you get drafted. Into the Army, you know? You don't have a choice. They make you—"

She puts her finger to your lips. "No talk," she whispers. "You listen. I tell story."

Another story? Will it be another old Vietnamese story, like the first one? That would be good. You like her stories.

She whispers into your ear:

"Man catch soft-shell turtle. Bring turtle home to eat. Tell servant girl kill turtle. Cook turtle for supper. Man go away. Servant girl get out knife. Start water boil. But turtle talk. Say, Please no kill. I hurt no one. Eat no flesh. Eat only green plant next to river. Please let go. Someday you get reward. Girl have knife in hand. Girl not know what to do. Master say want eat turtle for supper. Turtle say, Please. Take to river. Servant girl look at knife in hand. Throw down knife. Hide turtle in sack. Take to river. Let turtle go into water. When master find out, he very angry. He tell girl go away from house. Never return. Poor servant girl thrown out on street. Only clothes on back. Man tell neighbors not hire girl. Girl have no place to go. Cold rain come. She go to river to hide under wooden bridge. Girl have no food to eat. No blanket. She get very cold. She get very weak. She get sick and have terrible fever. She sure she going to die. Turtle come up out of water. See girl under bridge. Turtle cover girl with mud. Special mud from bottom of river. Make girl warm. Turtle bring girl fine green water plant and good white water root to eat. Girl feel better. People see turtle help girl by river. Bring other people to see. It miracle, they say. Master of girl come. He see miracle too. He say he sorry. He take girl back to house and let her be like daughter. He tell people he never eat turtle again."

She is staring into your eyes. What is that look? A question? Is she asking if you understood the story? Did you? It was a story about being kind to animals. Okay, it was a nice story, but why did she tell you *that* story? Did it have something to do with that thing she said about you being in danger?

You try to think of something to say, anything to make her happy. "Nice story," you say. "Poor little servant girl. She got thrown out, and then she got sick. Not fair. All she did was save a —"

Again, she puts her delicate little finger to your lips. "You listen." Her eyes are urgent. "Time come, they say kill. You must not kill."

What a strange thing to say. Does it mean you're supposed to be like the servant girl and not kill poor little animals? Nothing wrong with that idea. Being kind to animals is probably part of their Buddhist tradition.

But wait, what if she's not talking about killing things like turtles? What if she's talking about killing people? Like maybe killing some of her Vietnamese people?

You stare into her dark eyes to try to figure out what her story meant. But those eyes have no answers.

So dark, so intense, those eyes. What do those eyes want from you? A promise? But doesn't she know you're a soldier? Soldiers are supposed to kill the enemy when they are told to, and the enemy *is* people, even though they say a good soldier isn't supposed to think about that.

You want to ask her questions about what she meant, but before you can speak, she lies back down next to you and says, "No talk now. You sleep."

She wants you to sleep. But you don't want to sleep. You don't want this night with this beautiful girl to end with sleep.

You don't want to go to sleep, but your eyelids are feeling very heavy. Maybe you should close your eyes, just for a few minutes.

You open your eyes. It is still dark.

Something is wrong, very wrong. Your sleepy peacefulness is gone, and you are sweating. Why are you sweating? Are you afraid? Why are you afraid?

Then you remember, you are in Vietnam, a very long way from home. You were in a bar. You took drugs. There was booze. You drank too much booze. You ended up under a table.

You were brought to a back room with . . . Wait! There was a girl, a beautiful young girl! Is she still here? You reach out into the darkness, but your hands find nothing but the wadded-up pillow. The sweat-stained pillow is trying to deny that she was ever here. It's trying to tell you she wasn't real, that you dreamed her. Can that be? But everything seems so real, the night, the room, the noises coming from the street outside: shrill voices arguing, a dog barking in the distance, a motorbike passing with harsh overconfident loudness. So she had to be real too, didn't she? She told you stories. She was naked. So slim. So enticing. Wasn't she in this very bed, right here next to you?

But if she really was here, why did she go away? The room seems sad and empty and dark without her. Wasn't there flickering candlelight? And a little carved Buddha? She took the candlelight and the Buddha away with her, so now there's nothing left but the darkness and the emptiness.

You try to sit up, but you can't do it. You just don't have the strength. You lie back, out of breath. You stare up into the darkness. You have to try to think this through. You're in Saigon, Vietnam, a strange and fearsome foreign country. But *why* are you here? You have to put the pieces of the puzzle together. Use your brain. Think. Okay, you are in the Army. You got sent to this place, a place you shouldn't be.

But wait! Didn't *she* say that? Yes! *She* said you shouldn't be here. Somehow she knew you don't belong here. But how did she know? How could she know how wrong and pointless it all is? The war. Pointless. Us Americans being here. Wrong. You pretending to be a soldier. Wrong *and* pointless.

But if you aren't a soldier, what are you? Well, she showed you what you are, a make-believe soldier in a make-believe war. How could you not have seen it before?

The whole idea of being a soldier was a mistake, and somehow she knew it. The stupid idea overtook you that night you were sleeping on the ground out in the Arizona desert after yet another one of your long solitary hikes. It came to you in the middle of the night as you stared up at the infinite array of stars. You were shivering from the cold, and the moody desert sounds were talking to you about your wasted life, your pointless existence, your reliance on drugs and alcohol to make meaning out of it all. Those night sounds convinced you that you should do something worthwhile, like maybe you should join the Army. You were going to get drafted pretty soon anyhow, so why not go fight the Communist off there in that Vietnam place they are always showing on the TV.

The next morning, the cold clear reality of pragmatic cactus plants and restless coyotes tracks all around your campsite made the idea seem real, even logical. At least your life would have a purpose.

So you volunteered for the draft. You went through Army training, and before you even had a chance to think about what you'd done, they sent you here.

And for a while, it worked. You had a new purpose in life. You were in a strange, but interesting, new country. There was a war, but you were in no real danger. All you had to do was work in the supply warehouse all day and then go out drinking every night.

But then a strange girl got inside your mind and took everything away. She left you empty. Empty of purpose. Empty of expectations. Anything you had, or thought you had, before is gone. Your dream of being a heroic soldier going off to fight in a glorious foreign war has been revealed for what it was, a naive self-delusion, a childish fantasy. You are nothing but what you have always been, directionless, confused, unsure of yourself, often depressed, and now stuck for at least a year in Vietnam, the last place one earth you should be.

But there is one thing she can't take away from you—the solution. All you have to do is admit that your stupid life is just going to get worse and worse, so you can finally give up your ridiculous hopes and fantasies and pour enough strong Vietnamese booze into your body and inhale enough strong Vietnamese pot smoke into your lungs to finally convince your brain that you are serious about not wanting to do this stupid reality anymore so it will finally oblige by shutting the whole damn thing down to the extent that you can once again be absolutely sure that nothing matters at all, not even a strange Vietnamese girl who might not have even been real anyhow.

4

Writing the Third-Person Story

A third-person story is a story narrated by an unknown and unknowable storytelling "voice" that is not a participant in the story. The third-person storyteller's role is simply to convey information about the story to the reader. Unlike the narrator of a first-person or second-person story, the narrator of a third-person story should not have a recognizable "voice."

TIP:

If a story is told by an outside narrator that *does* have a "voice," it is known as a first-person **peripheral narrator**. Such stories are narrated by a person who *does not play a role in the story*, but *does* know the facts of the story.

If you decide to write a peripheral narrator story, there is one caution: it is harder for readers to get vicariously involved with a first-person narrator that is not part of the story.

When writing in third-person, the problem of narrator unreliability goes away. The third-person narrator, the storytelling "voice," is considered to be a reliable source of information about the world of the story.

In fiction writing, *omniscience*, is a third-person *concept* that does not necessarily mean the same thing as the dictionary definition of the word (infinite knowledge). In fiction writing, there are *degrees of omniscience*. A third-person narrator *can* know anything and everything about the world of the story; the narrator *can* know what happened in the past, and *can* even know what is going to happen in the future. An omniscient narrator *can* also know everything about every character in the story, including what they all are thinking.

Notice the emphasis of the word "can." Although a third-person narrator *can* know all these things, it is not a necessary aspect of third-person storytelling. When writing a story in third-person, you can *limit* what your narrator knows.

These days, it is common for writers to very strictly *limit* what the third-person narrator knows. Often, the narrator's character knowledge will be limited to only *what the protagonist knows*. This is sometimes referred to as third-person "close." In such stories, the third-person narrator *will* still know what the protagonist is thinking and *will* still report those thoughts to the reader, but such a narrator will only have the protagonist's knowledge of the world of the story. Also, the narrator will only know as much about the other characters in the story as the protagonist knows. That kind of limited omniscience gives a story the "feel" of a first-person story.

Getting the Story Started

So, how should we begin our example third-person story? We could use the "close" version that was described above, but in order to demonstrate all the capabilities of third-person, and to demonstrate some techniques we haven't covered so far, I will create a third-person example story that uses a narrator that is *somewhat* limited. How about we give our narrator knowledge only of events within the time frame of the story. That means the narrator won't know what is going to happen in the future. And let's limit the narrator's access to the *direct* thoughts of only one character. That means we can still portray *narrator-mediated* thought in the supporting-cast characters.

TIP:

When writing in third-person, there are two ways to convey a protagonist's thoughts to the reader. You can use the third-person narrator to move the reader's awareness *into* the protagonist's thoughts, as if the reader is "hearing" them. I refer to that as **direct thought**. It's as if the reader has been given access to the protagonist's "inner voice."

Compare that to what I refer to as **narrator-mediated thought**, which is when I use the third-person narrator to *summarize* the protagonist's thoughts.

There are other terms that are sometimes used to refer to these techniques, but I like these two terms because they remind you, the writer, of what you are doing.

As before, let's begin the story-creation process by imagining a character.

How about a street-wise character? Such characters are always interesting. We can make him even more interesting if we make him a bit of a hothead. That way, his contentious style of dealing with the world is bound to get him into trouble.

As you can see, coming up with an interesting character already starts to lead us toward a certain type of story.

Also, to demonstrate a variety of third-person techniques, let's make this a multiple-character story.

Unlike the previous two stories that focused on only one or two characters, a multiple-character story will force us to come up with names for the main characters so the reader can tell which one of them is acting or speaking.

First, we need a name for our protagonist. I searched the internet for a male name that "sounds" like a contentious character that might get himself into trouble, and the best name I've come up with (so far) is "Clint." It's an abrupt one-syllable name that sounds vaguely cow-boyish. Let's see if we can make our protagonist *act like* a character named Clint.

Many writers struggle with character names. I usually don't give my characters names until I've pretty much finished with the story. That's because I don't want to start thinking of my characters as hav-ing any particular name until I really get to "know" them. When I do name characters, I tend to give them *one or two-syllable names*. No particular reason except such names are easy for readers to pronounce and remember.

When I'm ready to find names for my characters, I go to the inter-net and look at lists of names. Baby naming sites are a good place to look for first names. If you are writing a story that is set in an earlier period, be aware that many names have not been around all that long. There are internet sites that list the most popular names for any period in history.

Also, different cultures and different parts of the United States have different naming conventions. A name like Buford might be common in the South, but rare in New York City. That kind of infor-mation can also be found on the internet.

I try to find names that "sound like" the characters. It's hard to explain exactly what I mean by that, but when you're ready to start looking for character names, keep an open mind and sooner or later you'll run across one that just *sounds right*.

However, you don't want to get locked into a name that won't sound right to the reader. If you sign up for a writing workshop, you can get reader feedback on character names as well as general feed-back on your writing. The names I chose for characters in my latest novels were tested in writing workshops. In my novel, *My Vietnam War*, I chose the name "Scott" for the protagonist because it seemed like a non-threatening kind of name that matched the personality of my protagonist. In addition, the name can be modified to the more familiar "Scotty." When other characters in the novel gradually start to get friendlier with the protagonist, I have them almost uncon-sciously start calling him Scotty.

In that novel, I chose the one-syllable name "Brent" for his pal, a big guy who is a clever drug dealer. To me, Brent sounds like a no-nonsense name that a tough drug dealer might have.

In my novel. *Psalm for Cock Robin*, I gave my protagonist the name "Harp" (given name, Harper). It's not only a one-syllable name, but it's also easy to remember because it's the name of a musical instrument. In fact, I have one of the supporting-cast characters in the book say, "Your name is Harp? Like what the angels play?" I wanted the reader to see Harp as innocent, to the point of being angelic. The name also ties in with his mother's many apocryphal Biblical refer-ences in the book. I gave other characters in that novel similarly evocative names. Speel is a poet who wanders around Venice Beach spouting his short clichéd poems. Paddy runs the poochmobile hot dog stand. Bailey, who does a sidewalk balancing act, became "Bai-ley the Balancing Man."

In my novel, *The Pain Artist*, the local gang leader has a tough reputation. I assigned him the gang name of "The Dog" and gave him a tattoo of a snarling pit bull with big teeth and startling red eyes. But he turns out to actually be a pretty nice guy, so also I gave him a tra-ditional and mainstream (but somewhat tough-sounding) name of "Jake." I named the girl interest in that book "Lilly" because she was beautiful, but psychologically fragile.

In my Drew Steele detective novels, the detective protagonist chose the professional name "Drew Steele" for himself because it "sounded like" a sharp detective's name. I gave his klutzy, out-of-shape assistant (he is the foil character in the story) the name "John Rudd" because it sounds like the kind of name a good-hearted fellow with limited capabilities might have.

Some writers choose names related to real-world objects like Spade or Bell. Some choose color names like Green or Gray, or occupation names like Cook or Hunter.

Whatever name you choose, try to come up with something that conveys to the reader the feeling or image or occupation you want to convey.

Even completely made-up names can bring an image to mind. Charles Dickens was a master at that, repeatedly coming up with fanciful names that somehow conveyed character personalities (Lady Honoria Dedlock, Luke Honeythunder, Mercy Pecksniff, and Fanny Squeers).

TIP:

Often, male characters in stories are referred to only by their last names. Throughout my LA noir novel, *Crueltown*, the two main characters are referred to as "Steele" and "Rudd."

But referring to female characters in fiction by their last names is unusual. Don't ask me why.

Okay, where should we start this story about a hot-tempered, street-wise character? How about we make it a prison story? We could say our protagonist's attitude has landed him in prison.

If prison is to be our *setting* for this third-person story, do we start with backstory to show what he did to get himself put into prison, or should we start with him already in prison?

The answer to that question depends on how important the incident was that got him into trouble. If it was a significant event, some writers might start the story with a bit of prologue-like backstory, creating a scene that shows him getting into trouble with the law.

But in this case, I'm thinking about creating a demonstration story that's centered around an attempted prison escape. Therefore, I think we should start with our protagonist already in prison.

Later, we can fill in backstory information about how he landed in prison.

Also, at some point (not yet), I'll have to come up with *a title* that ties in with the escape concept.

TIP:

Titles of stories can be used to provide clues to the reader about what the story is about. However, you shouldn't worry too much about a title as you start a story. It's actually better to wait until your story is complete. Why? For the same reason you shouldn't worry too much about what all the story events will be as you start a story. Coming up with a title before you write the story tends to put constraints on where the story can go. Even if your plot doesn't change all that much, the outcome of the story might end up being quite different from what you originally had in mind. I can't tell you how many student stories I've read that have seemingly mysterious titles. If I ask the student writer why he or she chose that title, I will usually get some long-winded explanation about the original idea the student had, but then the story "got away from them" and the title ended up being a conceptual idea that couldn't be found anywhere in the story.

When you are ready to create your story's title, you should think of it in the same way you think about your story's opening; that is, something to get the reader interested.

Okay, if we have a character and a setting, we can now look for a potential *opening scene*. Let's say our protagonist, being an irascible character, is not about to sit patiently in a prison waiting for his release date. No, he will look for a way to escape.

I don't think we should make it a high-security prison. That would lead us into spending a lot of words detailing a complex escape plan, and that could become plot-driven.

Instead, let's create a character-driven story about an attempted prison escape from a minimum security prison, one in which all a prisoner would have to do is wait for the right moment and then make a run for it. That should give us an interesting *situation*, one that will test our protagonist's capabilities, and at the same time, reveal any personal weaknesses that might make him fail.

Now that we have the initial elements of a story, we *could* start by taking the reader inside the protagonist's head to show what he's thinking about his situation. But since this demonstration story is to be an exploration of third-person techniques, let's start by using our third-person narrator to show what our protagonist is doing *and* what he is thinking.

> **Clint walks the fenceline. He's waiting for his chance to make a break for it.**
>
> **Inside his brain, there is a terrible heat. The heat is fueled by anger and resentment. It burns, day and night. It drives him, makes demands of him.**

This opening segment lets the reader know a character named Clint is walking along a fence and that he is looking for a chance to "make a break for it," whatever that means.

Most importantly, it puts the reader's focus squarely on Clint, our protagonist. The second paragraph puts the reader "in his mind." That should send a signal to the reader right off the bat that this story is going to be about what motivates this character named Clint.

The opening segment lets the reader know the protagonist has a heat inside of him that is fueled by anger and resentment. What is that "heat" going to drive him to do? The reader will have to keep reading to find out.

TIP:
Readers will assume that the **first character introduced** is going to be **the protagonist**.

Fiction writers sometimes take too much time establishing the situation. They may even introduce supporting-cast characters before they introduce the protagonist. I would advise against that. You want readers to get vicariously involved with your protagonist as soon as possible, so start that process right at the beginning of your story.

As we have seen, the main purpose of an opening paragraph of a story is to get the reader to continue reading. Therefore, I'm starting right out using the "wait for it" technique. The idea is to not only make the opening scene interesting enough to make the reader want to turn to the next page, but also to arouse questions in the reader's mind (What is this character angry and resentful about? What is this place that he wants to make a break from?).

TIP:
Writers sometimes begin their stories by **over-explaining**. They will over-describe the characters and over-describe the situation before they put their main character into action. The problem is, they have the whole story in their mind, so they tend to start *telling* the whole story right away instead of allowing the reader (and themselves) to "discover" it.

It might seem like I'm jumping right into the middle of the story. The protagonist is already in prison, already looking for a way to escape. If this is to be a character-driven story, why didn't I start at the beginning and show what he did to end up in prison?

The fact is, this is not the middle of the story. I want this story to be *about* a man trying to escape from prison, so my opening paragraphs starts with him thinking about escaping. To start the story with him getting arrested would make it a story about a man getting arrested, going to trial, and getting sent to prison, instead of a story about a prison escape attempt.

TIP:
Containment is one of the keys to creating a tight *short story*. If this was to be a novel, I probably *would* start at a point much earlier in the protagonist's life. But if I tried to do that in a short story like this, it might feel like the story's events were "wandering" toward the story's central issue, escape. To the reader, the escape attempt would be of equal or lesser value than the backstory of how he ended up in prison.

Okay, we have our opening scene. What's next? As we have seen, it's usually best to provide the reader with more information about the protagonist right at the start of the story, and one of the best ways to do that is to put the reader inside his head.

Let's do that.

> **As he paces along next to the fence, Clint can't stop thinking about how he got railroaded into this place. Plead guilty, they said, and you'll get a deal. Get a reduced sentence. Get to serve your time on the honor farm.** *Some deal. Two to five. Not fair. The guy didn't even die for Christ's sake. They call this place an honor farm, but it's still a damn prison. Locked up at night. A guard up in his wooden tower, rifle in his hands. That makes it a damn prison, whatever they wanna to call it.*

Here, after putting the reader *in the scene*, I used the *topic sentence approach* to put the reader "inside" our protagonist's head. Then, from that point on, I'm using italicized direct thought.

TIP:

Sometimes writers use **italics** to indicate *direct thought*. However, italics are supposed to be used for emphasis. Therefore, I would advise against writing very long passages of direct thought in italics. The longer italicized direct thought goes on, the more likely it is that the reader will think it doesn't *sound like* actual human thought. Better to reserve italics for its traditional purpose, emphasis.

For example, you might want to use italicized thought to emphasize how dramatic a thought is (*Oh my God, he's got a gun!*)

In this story, I'm going to use italics for protagonist direct thought to help you see the difference between direct thought and narrator-mediated thought.

Direct thought makes it seem like the reader is "hearing" the actual thoughts of the protagonist. It's about as close to first-person as you can get in a third-person story.

TIP:
Early in the twentieth century, modernist writers like Dorothy Richardson, James Joyce, Virginia Woolf, and William Faulkner began trying to find ways to portray actual thought more accurately. They used a technique called **stream of consciousness** in which long passages of a character's thoughts were depicted in a continuous flow. This type of *interior monologue* was intended to replicate the way humans think, including the randomness, interruptions, and changes of direction that are common to actual thought.

Today, some aspects of the stream of consciousness technique have found their way into modern short story writing, but conveying long sections of text that try to portray realistic-sounding thought patterns is still not very common in mainstream literature.

These first few paragraphs of our story not only provide the reader with information about what the protagonist is thinking, they also provide information about where he is (on an honor farm).

Then, by again giving the reader access to our protagonist's thoughts, we have given the reader a hint about how he ended up in prison (something to do with a guy who didn't *even* die). These kinds of story hints are another way to keep the reader involved in the story.

This opening segment also tells the reader that the prisoners are locked up at night. So, if Clint is walking along next to the fence, that means it's not night yet.

The protagonist's thoughts also tell the reader that there is a wooden tower with a guard who is armed with a rifle in his hands. As always, bringing a gun into the story foreshadows the potential for danger.

Now, that we have our story started, we have a number of choices. We can continue to give the reader access to our protagonist's thoughts, or we can have him engage in more action.

Dialogue is also a valuable tool that can be used to characterize a protagonist, but I can't use the dialogue tool now because I've placed him in a situation where he is alone.

TIP:
Writing long passages when the protagonist is alone is one of the more challenging tasks a fiction writer can be faced with. It precludes the use of the dialogue tool. That's why I created schizophrenic protagonists in two of my novels, ***Psalm for Cock Robin*** and ***The Pain Artist***. It gave me a way to use the dialogue tool even when my protagonist was alone.

Another way to use a form of the dialogue tool is to have your protagonist talk out loud to himself. I wouldn't recommend that unless you're trying to imply that the character is a little "off." If you've ever heard people talking to themselves, didn't it make you wonder if they were a bit odd?

Another option at this point in the story is to bring in the supporting cast. To demonstrate how to use supporting-cast characters in this example story, I think I'll make two of the other prisoners aware of what Clint is up to.

> **Supper is over, and the two old trustees are sitting on the bunkhouse porch watching Clint prowl along the fenceline. They look at each other and nod in agreement: Clint will run, and tonight will be the night. They smoke their cigarettes and wait for it.**

Here, I'm using the third-person narrator to introduce two supporting-cast characters. The narrator has some *omniscience* to know what is in the minds of these two new characters.

As you can see, I'm using the narrator-mediated thoughts of the two "watcher" characters to let the reader know that others are watching Clint, and that they know what he is up to.

It's somewhat unusual to have two characters think the same thought, but in this case, I'm trying to imply that the other prisoners know what Clint is up to.

This is the first time I've switched point of view in one of these demonstration stories. In this case, it's necessary in order to demonstrate how to create roles for supporting-cast characters. Although this paragraph *does* switch the point of view, it still keeps the focus on the protagonist and on the main theme of the story, his escape attempt.

As I said, you shouldn't go into the POV of a supporting-cast character *unless there is a good reason for it*. In this case, there *is* a good reason for it: later, we are going to need someone to show how the prison population reacts after Clint starts his escape attempt and runs away.

I like to reuse characters, so now that I've brought these two characters into the story, I can find other uses for them later. When that time comes, I'll have to watch for an opportunity to further identify them, and maybe even give them some dialogue.

Here, I'm using the third-person narrator to inform the reader of where the two supporting-cast characters are physically located (they are sitting on the bunkhouse porch). The narrator then informs the reader of what the two trustees are doing (they are smoking and watching the protagonist).

But notice I did *not* have the two trustees *describe* Clint physically. It wouldn't be logical for them to do that because they would already know what he looks like.

Prison trustees are interesting characters because of their situation —being locked up like all the other prisoners, but also having some of the responsibilities of prison staff. What will the reader think of these two old trustees? They will probably be wondering what role they will play when Clint starts his escape attempt. Will they act like fellow prisoners, or like part of the prison management?

As I said earlier, when you are writing in third-person, you have the option of giving your narrator *omniscient* qualities. That means we *could* take the reader more deeply into the thoughts of the two trustees to have them provide some backstory about Clint's arrival at the prison farm and his reputation among the other inmates. But it's not a good idea to move the reader's focus too far away from the protagonist. Therefore, I will only show thoughts of the two trustees that are related to Clint's planned escape.

TIP:

When writing in third-person, there's a temptation to *overuse the narrator*.

When beginning writers discover the ease with which a third-person narrator can provide information to the

---

reader, it's tempting to take the easy way out and constantly use the narrator to *tell* the reader the story instead of *showing* the reader the story through action and dialogue and protagonist perception.

If you overuse the narrator, the information flow will be from narrator to reader. The reader's relationship will be with the narrator rather than with the protagonist, and that will end up making your readers dispassionately *observe* the protagonist instead of getting vicariously involved with him.

Now, it's time to introduce another supporting-cast character, one that will play an even more important role in the story than the two trustees.

> **Poor Billy is a young man who's bigger than most of the other prisoners, but he sometimes seems to act more like a child. Billy is also watching Clint. He's sitting in the dirt behind the edge of the bunkhouse playing with his little twigs. Billy likes to twist his little pieces of twigs together to make them into stick people. His twig people are being held inside a prison with a fence that's made out of bigger twigs. He likes to pretend his twig people are real, and only he has control over them.**
>
> **Billy likes Clint, even if nobody else does. He likes Clint because Clint is world-smart. Billy wishes he would have got the chance to go places and do things so he could be world-smart too. But no, he had to stay at home for his whole life and help his daddy with the hunting and fishing. He didn't even get to go to a school, not once. His daddy said, What would be the use a learnin how to read and write? Would it help you know where the crocs and the fish hide in the swamp? Would it help you track an animal through the forest?**

Next, let's give Billy some kind of relationship with Clint.

> **Billy thinks Clint is his friend because Clint once gave Billy a little bit of the food he stole from the kitchen. When Clint slipped the food to him, he'd said, "You didn't see nuthin, did you Billy? This will be our little secret, right?"**
>
> **Billy has kept their little secret since that day. Even when they lined everybody up and said nobody was gonna get to eat supper unless they fessed up about who took that food from the kitchen, Billy kept his mouth shut. Poor Billy is good at keeping his mouth shut. And he's good at watching too.**

This supporting-cast character is focused on our protagonist, just as all the other "watcher" characters are. But with him, I've spent a lot more words introducing him to the reader. I've given him a name and shown some of his odd behavior.

I've also provided the reader with some of Billy's backstory, including the fact that he was only taught hunting and fishing and tracking skills instead of book learning and that he knows about forests and swamps (we can use that later).

That level of introduction should tip off the reader that this character is going to be important to the story, and hopefully, they will remember the specialized skills we've given him.

To further characterize him and to fix him in the reader's mind, I created something of a personal relationship with our protagonist (Clint gave him some stolen food, and they now share that secret). The reader should now realize (if only subconsciously) that Billy's relationship with our protagonist is going to play a significant role in the story.

Notice also that I'm further cementing the relationship between Billy and Clint by inserting a bit of dialogue from the past.

It's never a good idea to have *too many main characters* in a short story. Many of the best stories have only one supporting-cast character in addition to the protagonist.

However, *walk-on characters*, like waiters and parking attendants don't count as *main* characters. While they may play important roles, if you follow my earlier advice and don't name them or characterize them, the reader will realize they are only there to "support" the story.

So far, in this story, we have three "watcher" characters, the two trustees and Poor Billy. I've tried to "tip off" the reader that the two trustees are *somewhat* important to the story, but they are not going to be all that important *to our protagonist*.

However, I've developed Billy more fully because I plan to use him as *a foil*. I'm thinking I will do something with the fact that Clint is experienced and sly and world-wise, while Billy is a simple country boy, uneducated in the ways of the outside world.

Now the reader also knows that Billy has some knowledge about rural environments that city-boy Clint does not have (it is a prison *farm*, after all, which suggests to the reader that it must be in a rural area).

Later, we can use Billy's knowledge of the rural environment (and Clint's lack of knowledge about it) as part of the plot.

TIP:

The role a **foil character** plays in a story is to contrast with the protagonist. The term comes from an old marketing practice of backing gems with foil in order to make them shine more brightly.

In order to bring out a particular protagonist trait, you can create a foil character who is markedly different from your protagonist. In some stories, it's a way to show the protagonist's special abilities.

For example in my *noir* murder mystery novel, *Crueltown*, I created a foil character to contrast with my detective protagonist. He is a good-hearted fellow who tries hard but clearly does not have the detective's crime-solving abilities.

We're almost finished introducing supporting-cast characters into our story. However, we need to add one last "watcher" character, the guard in the tower.

He is something of an *antagonist* to our protagonist in that if Clint is going to be successful in his escape attempt, he's going to have to overcome the danger presented by the guard with his rifle.

TIP:

An **antagonist** is someone that threatens to thwart the protagonist.

You may think of an antagonist as a *villain*, but that is not necessarily true. A villain may do bad things in a story, but unless the villainy is directed at the protagonist, the villain is not actually an antagonist.

In fact, an antagonist doesn't even have to be a bad person; the antagonist may simply have a role in the story that is in conflict with the goals of the protagonist.

To let the reader know what the guard thinks of our protagonist, let's give him some narrator-mediated thought.

> **The guard in the tower is also watching Clint. He's seen it before: when one of the prisoners starts to pace next to the sagging barbed-wire fence, it means he's thinking about making a run for it. Even though the guard assumes a wiry-thin guy like Clint is probably pretty fast, he knows nobody is faster than a bullet, so he keeps his rifle in his hands, the safety off.**

So far, the reader knows nothing about the guard in the tower, other than the fact that he stands in Clint's way in his attempt to escape. The guard may dislike Clint or he may admire him, but regardless of his feelings about our protagonist, his job is to stop him from escaping.

The guard's thoughts provide the reader with more information about the situation *and* a bit more information about our protagonist (he is wiry-thin, and presumably, fast). In addition, by creating a guard character that stands in the way of our protagonist's goals, I've introduced a new plot issue: will our protagonist be able to overcome the obstacle of the guard—or more accurately, the guard's rifle—in order to successfully escape? And if Clint does escape, will the guard go after him and catch him? Let's stick with the guard's POV to give the reader a little more information.

> **He suspects Clint will wait until it gets a bit darker, and then, just before the prisoners get called in for nighttime lockup, he'll make a run for it.**

The narrator-mediated thoughts of the guard tell the reader about the danger to our protagonist and a bit more about the environment (it's getting dark). The guard believes Clint will probably make a run for it just before "the nighttime lockup." That puts a time limit on Clint's escape attempt: if he is going to try to escape on this day, he will have to go soon.

I am not providing any personal information or backstory about the guard. If I don't name him or even describe him, that should tell the reader that he is simply going to play the role of "guard."

TIP:

There is an old rule in fiction: if you **bring in a gun**, it better get used in some way. The gun, once it appears, needs to have a role in the story. It doesn't mean anybody has to get shot, but it does mean you should have a good reason for introducing it. A gun is sure to capture the reader's attention, but it is also symbolic of violence and control. In this case, the role of the guard's rifle is obvious: it presents a dangerous obstacle standing in the way of our protagonist's plan to escape.

The guard is our fourth "watcher" character, the only one that presents a threat to our protagonist. That threat adds plot, and the potential for considerable *drama*.

TIP:

A basic rule in fiction writing is that you should always be looking for ways to bring *drama* into the story. It's a useful guideline, but one that's often used inappropriately. Some writers bring "**false drama**" into their stories.

You see a lot of false drama in movie scripts, car chases and such. But in fiction, drama should make a contribution to the story. What is the point of yet another car chase if it doesn't characterize the protagonist or move the plot forward? What is the point of having your protagonist jump out of a third-story building and land on top of a moving bus without even suffering a sprained ankle? Such heroics may thrill moviegoers, but in fiction, it can turn your character into a cardboard cutout. If doesn't characterize the protagonist or add a plot complication, it's only false drama.

But there are ways to bring that kind of excitement into your story in a way that *does* move the plot forward. My *Crueltown* novel starts with a wild car chase and shootout. I used it as a dramatic way to introduce the capabilities of both my protagonist and his specially-built car, but it also becomes an important part of the plot because it presents the reader with a major plot question: are the shooters in the chasing car trying to kill the protagonist, or are they after the wife of the murdered man who is also in the car? And if they are trying to kill the murdered man's wife, why? Does it mean there is more to her husband's murder than meets the eye?

Dreams are another form of false drama that should usually be avoided in fiction. Writers often put their protagonist into what seems like a dramatic life-threatening situation, only to have them wake up. Only then does the reader find out it was just a dream. That kind of false drama is bound to make readers feel cheated. If a dream is important to your story (perhaps as foreshadowing or as a characterization technique), it would be better to have your protagonist wake up and think through the dream.

The fact that the guard is watching Clint, and believes he is going to try to escape, sets the stage for a battle of wits between Clint and the guard. Let's inform the reader of Clint's thoughts about that.

> **Clint knows the guard is watching him closely, but he's been watching the guard closely too. He's learned that the guard puts down his rifle whenever he lights a cigarette. He cups his hands around the match to protect it from the wind, even if there is no wind.** *The next time he puts down the rifle to light his cigarette, that'll be when I go.*

This protagonist thought about watching the guard tells the reader that Clint is watchful and that he has a plan.

I've now established all of the main players in the story. The reader is "getting to know" the protagonist, they know who the "watcher" characters are, and they know Clint has a plan to escape. Now, let's further characterize the two trustees and have them speculate about our protagonist.

> **Back on the porch, the senior trustee, the one with the full head of white hair (that he's quite proud of), says, "I'm tellin ya, tonight is the night. He's a gettin ready to run. And once he goes, he'll be fast."**

Here, I inserted a bit of dialogue to let the reader know what the trustee is thinking. I also use our third-person narrator to parenthetically insert some information about him (he is quite proud of his full head of white hair). I'm doing that to characterize him. It will help fix the man in the mind of the reader.

TIP:
Using a third-person narrator to parenthetically insert story information is not an especially common technique, but it can be effective in this kind of situation. Although it might be seen by some readers as metafiction (drawing the reader's attention to the fact that they are reading a work of fiction), most will probably see it as just another aspect of the narrator's omniscient capability.

I used *the dialogue tool* to let the reader know what the white haired trustee thinks about Clint's chances of escaping. It informs the reader that the trustee thinks Clint can move fast. That might, in the reader's mind, make it a bit more likely that Clint might actually be able to escape.

TIP:

As I said earlier, **dialogue** is one of the most valuable tools in the fiction writer's tool kit. Dialogue brings a sense of immediacy to any story, as if the reader is "eavesdropping" on the conversation. In a character-driven story, you probably won't want to "go inside" the mind of a supporting-cast character using direct thought, so the use of dialogue is a good way to inform the reader what such characters might be thinking.

Another good guideline regarding dialogue is to make each speaker sound somewhat different, from each other. You should be able to tell which character is speaking simply by the way they talk or what they talk about. Think about the dialogue in your story as if it is being spoken in a play on stage. If the stage lights suddenly went out and the play went on, could you tell which character was speaking?

Now let's insert a brief description of the other trustee and give him some dialogue that will tell the reader more about what our protagonist is up against.

> "Yeah, well, that may be," says the one-eyed trustee, taking a big draw off of his loose-rolled cigarette, "but (here he points to the west with his cigarette-yellowed first finger) how's he think he's gonna get through the swamp? He may be fast, but that won't help him one bit once he's got hisself in that damn swamp. Man's gotta have a boat to get through that swamp. Otherwise, crocs. And snakes. Don't forget bout them crocs and them snakes."

Through the use of dialogue, we have now informed the reader of yet another danger to our protagonist (a swamp with crocs and snakes).

TIP:

When using dialogue in your stories, make sure the reader always knows who is talking. Whether you are using a pronoun like 'he" or "she," a name, or as in this case, some identifying characteristic, don't go overboard on the complexity of the *dialogue tags* you use. Mostly, you will want to use "says" (in present tense) and "said" (in past tense). Creating fanciful dialogue tags like "he beamed" is attempting to use the narrator to "tell" the reader what the character looked like when he spoke. But how can words beam? It works a lot better to let the protagonist take note of how the character spoke (Jane noticed that his greeting was accompanied by a broad smile. What was he so happy about?). That way, the reader still gets the information, but they stay vicariously involved with your protagonist. If you want a character to display some kind of emotional affect as he or she speaks, and it's important to the story, don't waste it with a phony dialogue tag that's actually an abrupt narrator statement to the reader.

I've briefly described both of the trustees and provided the reader with some information about their relationship. The white-haired trustee appears to be older and more experienced than the trustee described as one-eyed.

TIP:

There will be times when you need to identify supporting-cast characters, but you don't want to give them a name because they aren't going to play a significant role in the story. In such situations, I recommend identifying them by some notable characteristic that fill fix them in the reader's mind.

Once you've identified your characters, you should try to differentiate them by how they use language—through their word choices, their use of colloquialisms, or the way they structure sentences. In addition, there are regional and cultural dialects that can be used to characterize speakers.

In this segment, I've had both trustees use language in a way that characterizes them. For example, I've consistently dropped the "g" from the end of their "ing" words. Although today's readers might get tired of continual indications of most types of dialect, dropping the "g" is so common in fiction these days, I'm using it throughout this example story. I've also given them other region-specific language patterns, like adding the letter "a" before the use of the word "gettin" and hisself instead of himself.

As we go forward with this story, let's have Clint and Billy also use their own characteristic forms of dialect to indicate their backgrounds.

The dialogue between the two trustees informs the reader about a nearby swamp. By using the eavesdropping technique to bring a swamp and crocodiles and snakes into the story, I'm adding plot complications. They all represent potential danger related to Clint's planned escape. (At this point, the reader may also remember that some of Billy's skills relate to a swamp.)

I'm making sure the conversation between the two trustees is focused on Clint, but dialogue can also be used to characterize their relationship. Let's add a bit more dialogue to bring a new plot issue into the story.

> **"Yeah, there's crocs," says white-hair, "and they sure as hell is plenty snakes, but it won't matter to a runner like Clint. He don't care about crocs and snakes. He got to run, so run he will."**
>
> **"I got a half of a dollar and a quarter right here in my pocket," says one-eye. "My money says he won't make it through the swamp."**
>
> **"You bet I'll take that bet," says white-hair. "'He'll make it cause when he goes, it'll be quick, like a sudden wind at night, the kind of wind that wakes you up, but when you lie there lookin up in the dark, it's already done gone."**

Now, with money on the line, the two trustees are no longer passive observers. They've taken a stand on the outcome of Clint's escape attempt, and once the bet is made, they will both want to win. We can use that desire to win later in the story.

Now, let's add a bit more drama to the prospect of our protagonist trying to escape through a swamp. Let's continue to use dialogue and the eavesdropping technique to do it.

"Well, they can't make me chase after him," says one-eye. "Even my good leg is gettin bad now. And don't forget they got them trackin dogs. They don't need us."

"They'll make us go along," says white-hair. "You can count on it. And if he makes it to the swamp, they'll put us in a boat to go in there after him. Back before you got here, they made me a chaser. And let me tell ya, it was spooky out there all night in a boat. You could hear things movin in the water. Weird sounds, squawks and growls like I can't describe."

"Did you catch the guy?" asks one-eye.

"No, but we found his clothes. All bloody."

"Croc?"

"I spect."

With this concept of the dangerous swamp now fully fixed in the reader's mind, the stage is set for Clint to try to escape.

By bringing in the threat of the guard and the specter of a failed prior escape attempt that was doomed because of the swamp, I've stacked the odds against Clint surviving an escape attempt.

But will the reader think our protagonist is bound to fail? Readers, perhaps trained by years of watching heroes win against all odds in movies and books, don't generally believe protagonists are going to fail. But in this case, I've spent a lot of words characterizing the "watcher" characters. Will the reader think they will succeed, meaning the protagonist will fail? If you set the stage properly by showing how "driven" your protagonist is, an alternative character-driven plot *could be* how Clint reacts to failure.

With all that in place, let's take the reader back inside the mind of our protagonist to learn more about what he's planning.

> Clint knows that when it gets just a bit darker, it'll be time for the call-in. That means he's got to make his break for it pretty soon. It's taken weeks of study, but by now he knows every inch of the fenceline. He knows there is one place where the barb-wire fence is weak, a place where it sags low enough for a man to make it over in one quick movement. Now all he has to do is wait for the guard to put down his rifle to light his cigarette. It's been almost an hour since that guard's last fag, so he'll be needin one soon.
>
> Clint turns to look at the two old trustees that are sitting on the porch. *Those two are always watchin. But who cares about them. Two old lifers. Probably couldn't run down a three-legged dog if their life depended on it.*

Here, I'm using a combination of *narrator-mediated thought* (Clint knows) and *direct thought,* in italics, to let the reader know what our protagonist is thinking.

The reader now knows Clint's plan is to wait for the guard to put down his gun long enough to light a cigarette.

How do we show that happen, narrator or protagonist thought? It's tempting to use the narrator to just tell the reader (the guard lights his cigarette), but direct thought is more dramatic, and it lets the story continue to play out from within the protagonist's mind, so let's use that approach.

> *There's the flare of the guard's match. Time to go.*

As indicated by protagonist thought, Clint is ready to run. Now the story switches from a planned escape to an actual escape attempt. Will he make it over the fence and into the woods before the guard can react and pick up his rifle?

And how should we show the guard's reaction? We could switch to the guard's POV to show him seeing Clint make a break for it, but I don't want to let the reader get into a participatory role with the guard (remember, he is simply playing *the role* of guard).

But what about using the other two "watchers," the two trustees? That way, the reader can "watch" Clint's escape attempt play out, seeing what Clint does *and* what the guard does.

Let's use that approach and start the action with the sound of the gun.

> **The rifle shots bring the two trustees to their feet.**
> **"I can't see clear," says one-eye. "Did the guard get him?"**
> **"Don't think so," says white-hair. "No, now I see him. He's a runnin, and he's made it to the woods. Didn't I tell ya? Didn't I say he'd be fast?"**
> **"Yeah, but you ain't got my money yet. He still got to get through that swamp."**

By using the dialogue of my two "observer" characters, I can *report* the story action to the reader using the eavesdropping technique. By eavesdropping in on the trustee's dialogue, the reader now knows there were multiple rifle shots, but Clint made it to the woods.

Notice that I'm keeping the bet between the two trustees front and center. Why? Because I plan to use that bet later in the story. It's what I call the "murder mystery hidden clue" technique.

TIP:

The **"murder mystery hidden-in-plain-sight clue"** technique is not only useful in murder mysteries; it can be used in almost any type of story as a way to get information in that can be used later.

One of the reasons murder mysteries have long been popular is that readers like to try to analyze the clues right along with the protagonist-detective. In modern murder mysteries, it's the task of the writer to give readers all the clues, but still manage to slip the most important clues past the readers without them noticing.

In my *noir* murder mystery novel, ***Crueltown,*** an autopsy of the first murder victim reveals a broken condom inside the stomach cavity. The "experts" have seen that kind of thing before when swallowed condoms that were used to smuggle heroin into the

---

United States burst inside the stomach, killing the
smuggler by overdose. Therefore, at the autopsy,
everyone assumes the victim was a drug mule, and
further, that the murder had something to do with illegal drugs.

Actually, the condom in the stomach *does* turn out
to be a very important clue to the mystery, but it has
nothing to do with smuggled drugs. By bringing in
the observations of the "experts," the condom clue
leads the reader in the wrong direction.

The same sort of technique can be used in other
kinds of stories to bring important information into
the story without drawing undue attention to it. That
way, when the supposedly minor information turns
out to be very important to the plot, the reader can be
surprised.

Readers enjoy that kind of surprise, and it can be
used to add punch to the end of your story.

The reader now knows what the guard and the two trustees do in
response to Clint's escape attempt, but what about our other observer
character, Poor Billy?

I said earlier that I planned to use Billy as a *foil* character. That
means he has to somehow hook up with Clint.

Let's use the third-person narrator to take care of that.

> **What the two trustees didn't see in all the excite-
> ment, and what the guard who was climbing down
> from his guard tower didn't see, was that Poor Billy
> also took off. Over the fence and into the woods he
> went, chasing after Clint, like a dog chasing after his
> master.**

Here, I'm using the third-person narrator to inform the reader
about what Billy does.

I had to use the narrator to show it because none of the other characters in the story saw it.

TIP:

A significant advantage of telling your story in third-person is that it gives you the ability to use the narrator to pass information to the reader, even if nobody in the story has access to that information. If I was writing this story in first-person, Clint, the protagonist, wouldn't have seen Billy come after him, so he couldn't have reported that information to the reader. That would also be true if I was using the form of third-person that's limited to the perceptions of the protagonist. By using a *somewhat* more omniscient version of third-person, I can inform the reader of things I want them to take note of.

There is a potential problem with this approach: it puts the reader in the position of an observer, and they could lose some vicarious involvement with the protagonist. However, since this is a demonstration story, I wanted to show you some of the ways third-person omniscience can be used.

Now, let's get the reader back involved with the protagonist by using a combination of narration and protagonist thought.

Clint is sweating and breathing hard by the time he makes it into the woods, but his successful escape proves his plan was a good one. He heard shots, and he heard one of the bullets hit the ground behind him, but once he made it into the woods, there was no way that damn guard could get another shot off at him. He's not happy that his hands and knees got a bit cut up going over that damned barb-wire fence, but he tells himself not to worry about that; the bleeding will stop soon. The important thing is, he's free!

But no sooner does he have that thought when he realizes he'll have to keep running hard cause they'll soon be comin with their trackin dogs. He knows his only chance is to get to the swamp before the dogs come.

This time, I'm using the third-person narrator and narrator-mediated protagonist thought to report Clint's progress. It provides the reader with information about the environment (he made into the woods) and his physical condition (his hands and knees got cut on barb-wire). His thoughts also reveal that he's trying to get to the swamp before the dogs can catch him. That *foreshadows* what may happen next.

Now that we have our protagonist on the run, what should we do next? Should we show his progress by using more protagonist thought as he runs away, or should we switch back to the prison to find out how the watchers are reacting to his escape attempt?

And what about the Billy character? We've already informed the reader that he chased after Clint. Where is he now, and what is his role going to be if he catches up with Clint?

Let's bring Billy back into the story by having him catch up with Clint. Then we can use our third-person narrator to show how Clint reacts.

> **"Wait for me, Clint. You're running too fast."**
> **Clint is startled by the voice coming out of the darkness behind him. He turns to see who it is.**

This sets up an important moment in the story: how is Clint going to react to Billy following him? Let's show it with dialogue.

> **"What the hell ya think yer doin, Billy? You can't come with me. You gotta go back. And right now!"**
> **"But I don't want to go back, Clint. I want to go with you."**
> **"Well, ya can't. Where I'm goin, you don't wanna be. Now git!"**

With this bit of back-and-forth dialogue, we've established that Clint doesn't want Billy tagging along, but Billy doesn't want to go back.

Clint's dialogue indicates that he thinks he is the dominant personality. He thinks he can command Billy.

But will Billy do as he is told? One very subtle clue might be found in the difference between their use of language. I've made

Clint's language rough and imprecise, while Billy's language—even though he is supposed to be the one who is uneducated and maybe even a bit child-like—is more measured and grammatically correct.

The reader may or may not notice the difference in their speech patterns, but at some level, I'm hoping they will get the feeling that although Clint is aggressive and domineering, he is acting impulsively, while Billy's actions are more reasoned.

Since I'm using Billy as a foil character, I want the reader to notice their contrasting styles and personalities. The reader knows what Clint's plan is (simply to escape) and they know he has "a heat" that drives him. But what will the reader think Billy's motives are?

I want Billy's motives to be seen as simple and honest: he doesn't especially want to get away from the prison, he just wants to go along with whatever adventures Clint is going to find.

The different motives of the two characters have now become an aspect of the plot. The reader may even begin to suspect that although Clint is a strong and experienced loner, the success or failure of his escape attempt may, in the end, rely on Billy.

Now, I can use the narrator to show what Billy does next.

But Billy does not turn back. He just stands there staring down at his worn-out old shoes.

Now that we've begun to establish the relationship between these two characters, we can go back to using our protagonist's "inner voice" (direct thought) to show the reader what he plans to do about this unexpected turn of events.

Why did Poor Billy follow me? Musta seen me go over the fence and just followed. Like a dog followin a kid to school. What a dummy. Don't know nuthin about nothin. Born out in the country, I bet. For damn sure he's not a smart city guy like me. Probably never been anywhere out of this county til he ended up locked up in that prison farm. Probably got caught following somebody else when they went in to rob a store, or somethin like that. I'd better just ignore him and run faster. He'll never be able to keep up with me.

Here, I'm using protagonist direct thought to show his speculations about Billy. We want the reader to go along with these speculations and see it as actual backstory about Billy.

TIP:
Unless you have clearly shown your protagonist to be mistaken about his beliefs, readers tend to believe protagonist thought. Hard to say exactly why that is, but it's true. Maybe readers subconsciously realize the writer is passing them information through protagonist thought (otherwise, why is it in the story?).

The reader should now believe (or at least suspect) that Billy *is* an unsophisticated country boy who has never been to the big city, and that he probably ended up in prison because of his tendency to follow others (which they have now seen in action). As this story progresses, it's important that the reader sees Billy as a harmless young fellow who, despite the fact that he is incarcerated, is not actually a criminal.

The reader will now also know that Clint sees himself as a smart city guy. But will they believe he is actually all that smart? We want them to accept that he *has* been around, and that he *has* seen a lot, but his self-assessment may not be entirely *reliable*.

Now it's time to introduce a new concept into the story. Let's show Clint as unable to shake Billy no matter how fast he runs. Let's use three different tools to do that, dialogue, narration, and protagonist thought.

"I'm tired of running, Clint. Where we going?"
Clint is again startled to find that Billy is somehow keeping up with him. *Damn. How'd that big dummy even figure out which way I went? The last thing I need is him followin me.*

Notice that I didn't need to use the third-person narrator to tell the reader that time has passed. Instead, I used Billy's dialogue to show he is "tired of running" which *implies* it. I also implied the passage of time by using the third-person narrator to show that Clint is startled to see that Billy is somehow keeping up.

TIP:
In fiction, you have a variety of techniques that can be used to indicate time has passed. Some writers simply insert extra lines spaces. Sometimes there is no other way, but if you use that method, you should do it consistently to be sure the reader "gets it."

Clint seems to be running very fast, and yet, Billy is always right there behind him. This is not exactly *magical realism*, but it could be interpreted that way.

I often like to put a bit of the unexplained into my stories. It helps to get the reader to interact with the story on more than one level.

TIP:
Magical realism is a term that has been used since the 1950s to refer to the insertion of seemingly unreal elements into stories that otherwise seem realistic. If these types of unreal elements are integral to the plot, the story may come to be referred to as a "magical realism story." However, the role such magical elements play in a story can vary considerably.

My novel, *My Vietnam War*, has an important scene that could be seen as magical. A character in the story foretells what is going to happen to the protagonist in the future. When the future plays out in exactly the way it was predicted, the reader might wonder if it was magic, or whether the future-teller simply had advance knowledge of what was going to happen. There's no way to be sure what a reader might think, but the protagonist thinks about it as magical.

Alternatively, what might seem magical in a story could just be the protagonist seeing it that way. If so, the story wouldn't normally be called magical realism but would instead be seen as relating to the psychology of the protagonist.

Billy, who seems like a person who would be slower than Clint, somehow has the ability to find Clint no matter where he goes.

Billy seems to have a nearly unbelievable ability to get through the woods very quickly. Is it magic, or does Billy just know the lay of the land better? That issue will turn out to be important in this story.

Now, how do we show our protagonist's reaction to the fact that Billy is somehow able to keep up with him? Let's have him again try to get rid of Billy.

> **Clint stops and points back toward the prison farm. "Of course you're gettin tired, Billy. And I'm gonna be movin even faster from now on, so you won't be able to keep up. You'd best just go back now. So long, Billy."**

By now, the reader is probably not going to believe Billy will go back, no matter what Clint thinks.

Next, let's give Clint some direct thought that will hopefully also be seen by the reader as unreliable. His thoughts can also be used to remind the reader that the prison officials will soon be coming with their tracking dogs.

> *Billy will hafta go back now. Don't know why he followed me in the first place. Gotta keep movin. They'll be comin soon with those damn dogs.*

Now let's use our third-person narrator to show Clint going back to his fast running, and at the same time, provide a bit more information about the environment.

> **Clint leaves Billy standing there and goes back to running. Although a rusty gold moon has come up to hover just above the horizon, it's still very dark, so he often trips and falls. But each time, he gets up and continues on, cursing under his breath.**

We now need to move time forward again. As before, let's indicate the passage of time by giving Billy some dialogue and then show Clint's two-step response in the form of direct thought.

> **"Please, Clint, you're running too fast. I can't hardly keep up."**
> *Damn. He's still there. Doesn't seem to matter how fast I run, he's always right behind. How does he run so fast in the dark? If they catch me now, they'll think I dragged him along intentional.*

In addition to using the two-step as a response to Billy's presence, we also used protagonist thought to bring another issue into the story, Clint's concern that the authorities might think he intentionally dragged Billy along. Let's again use narration to show the reader how Clint reacts, and then we can follow that with dialogue to show how he again tries to get rid of Billy.

> **Clint stops and shakes his finger at Billy. "Now listen here, Billy. I'm headin for the swamp. You gotta go back now. I can't have you taggin along after me. You hear?"**

After Clint reveals his plan to go to the swamp, we can use dialogue to show how Billy might well be Clint's salvation.

> **"But this isn't the way to the swamp, Clint. You're going the wrong way."**
> **"The hell you say. They told me the swamp was straight west of the prison, and that's what I been doin. Goin west."**
> **Billy shakes his head. "I don't think this is the right way, Clint."**
> **"Now Billy, ya tellin me you think you know the way to the swamp?"**
> **"Sure, Clint. I was born and brought up around here. Right over . . . " He points. "That way."**

This bit of back-and-forth dialogue reveals a lot. It expands on the concept that although Clint sees himself in the leadership role, that belief may well be unreliable. He has been proceeding on the assumption that he knows exactly where he is going, but now he's being told he's wrong. But will he believe Billy, a young fellow he's been think-ing of as "a dummy"?

Now that Billy has revealed that he knows the area well, I'm hop-ing the reader will understand how he has been able to keep up with Clint.

This bit of dramatic irony (the reader knows that Clint is lost but Clint still doesn't realize it) is intended to begin the *character arc* process in which Clint has to learn how to switch from being the leader to being the follower if he is going to successfully escape.

TIP:

A challenge that every fiction writer must face is how often to use dialogue tags (he says, he asks, he whispers, he yells). As a general rule, you should use dialogue tags whenever there could be doubt about which character is speaking. You don't have to worry all that much about overusing dialogue tags because readers hardly notice them.

When there are only two characters in a scene and you are giving them back-and-forth dialogue, you can often get away with not using dialogue tags at all.

Another way to avoid using dialogue tags is to have characters use each other's name as part of the dialogue. (However, you should make sure that the style of verbal address "fits" the speaking style of the character.)

You can also identify a speaker by "leading in" to a line of dialogue with character action (Clint stops and turns back). If the dialogue begins in the same para-graph immediately after the action, readers will assume that the character that performed the action is the one doing the speaking.

So far, we have portrayed Clint as a man of action, but one who tends to make mistakes in judgment. Let's have him make another mistake by not believing Billy. (It also maintains the dramatic irony.) We'll convey it to the reader using direct protagonist thought.

> *Does this big dummy really think he knows his way around these woods in the dark? He's probably as lost as I am. They said the swamp was to the west, so I'll just keep runnin in that direction til I find it. Once they bring out the dogs, that swamp water'll cover my scent. And once I'm through the swamp and on the other side, I'll be home free. All I got to do is just keep on runnin.*

Our protagonist has failed to listen to Billy's advice about how to get to the swamp. It's time for him to learn that was a mistake.

> **"I been waiting here for you, Clint. I hear dogs. They're getting closer."**
> *Oh, no. I been runnin and runnin, and somehow Billy's got ahead of me. Have I been runnin in circles?*

Here, I'm using Billy's dialogue to indicate that some amount of time has passed. But this time, Billy hasn't been chasing, he's been waiting, which tells the reader that Clint has been running in circles and Billy knows it. Now, even single-minded Clint realizes it too.

Let's use a combination of back-and-forth dialogue, intermingled with protagonist thought to show how Clint is going to deal with this new awareness.

> **"I'm afraid of those dogs, Clint. What if they catch us?"**
> **"Pipe down, Billy. If you don't quit blabbin, they will catch us. Them dogs can hear talkin a mile off."**
> **Billy whispers, "I'm sorry, Clint. I'll be real quiet."**
> **"Now you got to tell me, Billy, do you really know the way to the swamp? You got to tell me true if you don't."**
> **"It's right over yonder, Clint." He points. "Not too far."**
> *Maybe he does know the way. I'm so lost, God help me if he don't.*
> **"I changed my mind, Billy. You can go with me. But we got to get to that swamp fore the dogs come.**

> How about you show me the way."
> *I'll let him lead me in the right direction, and then*
> *I'll git goin on my own. He won't be able to keep up*
> *with me, and then, when the dogs come, they'll go for*
> *him fore they get to me.*

It's time to get them to the swamp. Let's again show that by using dialogue and protagonist thought.

> "Here's the swamp, Clint. I told you I knew where it was."
> *By God, the dummy really did know the way. Now I can lose them dogs in the water. Gotta move fast.*
> "I know how to find the swamp cause me and my daddy used to come here crawdaddin. We'd put a piece of gristle meat on a string and—"
> "Sush, Billy. I got no time for your nonsense. You got me to the swamp, but best you go back now."
> "But, Clint—"
> "I said no! Didn't you hear me say no? Now git!"

Next, let's use dialogue to again move time forward. We can do it in a way that shows Billy didn't turn back. We can also use the dialogue tool to give the reader some sense of where they are.

> "Why do we have to be in this water, Clint? I'm cold."
> "Jesus, you scared me, Billy. You been followin me all this time?"
> "I'm sorry, Clint."
> "Of course you're sorry, cause you're cold. It's what you get for not doin what I said. You shoulda knowed it was gonna be cold in this damn swamp. You think I'm not cold too? When you're up to your ass in water hour after hour, you're gonna get cold, right? I told you to go back, but did you do it? No. So now you're cold. Too bad, but it's your own damn fault."
> "But I'm really cold, Clint. I'm shakin."

> "It's called shiverin, Billy. You don't think I'm shiverin too. It's natural when you get real cold. You got to be tough, like me. The sun'll come up by and by. Then, we'll be okay, long as the crocs don't get us."
>
> "There aren't any crocs left in this swamp, Clint. My daddy said he and his friends caught em all. For the meat."
>
> "Really? Well, thank heaven for that. It means I'm gonna make it. Ha! And they said I couldn't do it."
>
> "But there's land in the middle of this swamp, Clint. Why don't we go there?"
>
> "Land? Bull. There's nothin in this damned swamp but water and more water."
>
> "I know where there's land, Clint. Can't we go there?"
>
> "Well, if you think there's land in this godforsaken swamp, just show the way. But I'll believe it when I see it."

Now, we can briefly use the narrator and some dialogue to show them finding some dry land. It creates a new environment in which to develop a new scene.

> When Billy really does lead them to a small island of dry land in the middle of the swamp, Clint is amazed. "By God, Billy, you did find us a speck of dry land. Don't know how you find your way in the dark. Maybe you got them cat eyes."
>
> "It's always dry here, Clint. Me and my daddy used to come here fishin."

Now, for the first time, they can stop moving. It gives us a chance to let them get to know each other better.

> "That may be, Billy boy, but we got no time for fishin. We'd better just sit tight here and wait for the dawn. Them dogs won't be able to track us here with all that water around us."

This segment shows that Clint is becoming a little more friendly to "Billy Boy." (But he is not about to acknowledge Billy's help).

Now, instead of using the third-person narrator to show what is going to happen next, let's let our protagonist's thoughts show what he's planning to do.

> *Wind's picking up. Wet clothes. Too cold. Better dig a trench. Get down out of the wind.*

Then, we can use the dialogue tool for some back-and-forth conversation that also gives the reader more backstory information about Clint.

> **"Why you digging with that stick, Clint?"**
> **"Why you think, you ninny? I'm trying to get out of the wind. Leave me alone."**
> **"I can help you dig, Clint."**
> **"I don't need your help, Billy. Dig your own."**
> **"Can't I be in your hole with you?"**
> **"What? Are you queer or somethin'? Get away from me."**
> **"I just thought it'd be warmer for both of us."**
> **"Well, I don't want you anywhere near me. I don't need you to keep me warm. I don't need you for nuthin. I been on my own since I was twelve, and I never asked nobody for nuthin. Just leave me alone."**

We have now established a two-character scene using only dialogue. So, how should we have Billy respond to Clint's lack of appreciation? If we don't want to go into Billy's POV, we *could* use the third-person narrator. However, for the most part, I've managed to avoid much use of the narrator because we don't want the interaction to be between narrator and reader.

We *could* give Billy some dialogue to have him complain, but I've been trying to show him as a simple fellow who is, for the most part, uncomplaining.

Next, we can show Clint's observation of Billy.

> *So now he shuts up. Not a peep out of him. Just sits there starin at the ground, shiverin and poutin.*

Here, I used protagonist thought to describe what Billy is doing. Using protagonist thought to describe what other characters are doing is an underused application of the thought tool.

Now, let's continue using Clint's thoughts to give the reader a little more backstory.

> *Damn, it's cold in these wet clothes. How can it be so cold? I shoulda gone further south before I got myself throwd in jail. I coulda made it all the way to Florida if I hadn't a stopped. But no, I had to hop off that damn train in some backwater town, some hell-and-gone place with nuthin to do there cept get drunk. And then, that smart ass had to go and insult me. Okay, so I hit the guy. So what? I've hit lots of guys before, and none of em went and got themselfs checked into no hospital. A club, the cops said. Said I hit him with a club. A club? It wasn't no damn club. It was only a damn pool cue. You can't call a normal old pool cue a club.*

After the quiet moment of protagonist thought about how he ended up in prison, we can use a bit of narration to put Clint to sleep and show Billy's reaction to being left awake by himself.

> **Clint lets the heat and resentment of memory lull him to sleep,**
> **Billy stays where he is for a while, but soon grows so cold he has to creep closer to Clint to try to find a place out of the wind.**
> **Clint sits bolt upright and yells, "Croc!"**
> **"No, it's only me, Clint. I got too cold."**
> ***Jesus. It's only the dummy.*** **"Whatta think you're doin, Billy? Don't you ever touch me like that again when I'm asleep. You scared the hell out of me."**
> **"I'm sorry, Clint, I got real cold."**
> **"Well, I'm cold too. Damn cold. But didn't I tell**

> you to stay away from me?"
> "I'm sorry, Clint. I thought if we were in the same
> hole, we'd both be warmer."
> "Well, maybe that's so. Just maybe. But if you're
> gonna be in my hole, you can't move. You got that?
> You don't move a muscle til the sun comes up."
> "All right, Clint. Just let me get covered up, and
> then I won't move any more."

Now, we can again switch back to protagonist thought to show Clint's two-step reaction to what Billy is doing.

> *Now what's the ninny doing? Jesus, he's coverin*
> *himself up with dirt. Probably thinks he'll be warmer*
> *that way. What a dummy. Gettin himself all covered up*
> *in dirt.*
> *And now he's sound asleep. How can anybody go to*
> *sleep that fast, what with the cold and the wind and*
> *them dogs barking in the distance?*
> *But maybe covering himself up with dirt wasn't such*
> *a bad idea after all. Maybe I should try it. I'll be back in*
> *the water soon, and the dirt will all wash off anyhow.*

Gradually, Clint is learning from Billy, but he still is not showing any appreciation for it. More and more, the concept of Billy leading and Clint following is changing the story.

Previously, I described how a character-driven story's plot relates to character arc. But in this story, is our protagonist learning and growing? As we saw in the second-person story, after experiencing the events of the story, a protagonist may decide to resolutely stick to his old tried and true way of being. Will Clint end up doing the same? We need to move time forward again (using protagonist thought).

> *Damn the long night. Why does the night have to be*
> *so long? And so damn cold. Maybe I need some food in*
> *my stomach to warm me up.*
> **Clint carefully unwraps his secret stash of food,**
> **trying not to wake Billy up.**

Let's have the smell of food wake Billy up.

> "You got food, Clint?"
> "So you're awake now are ya? Slept like a baby, didn't ya? While I had to lay awake here all night keepin watch out for them crocs and them snakes. Well, all I got is a couple a near burnt up taters nobody else wanted. You wouldn't like em."
> "But I'm hungry, Clint."
> "Well, too damn bad. There's not enough for both a us."
> "Please, Clint."
> "You shoulda thought about gettin hungry fore you took off after me. I didn't ask you to come along, did I? Did you hear me askin you to come along? No. Now if you think I'm gonna share my food with you, you got another think comin."

Once again, if we don't want to turn Billy into a complainer, we can't use dialogue. I'll continue to use protagonist thought to describe what Billy is doing.

> *So now he's gone back to poutin again. Watchin me eat with his one stupid tear makin a track through the dirt on his face, all the way down to his chin. Looks like the trail a snail leaves when it walks across a fat red to-mater. Man, I wish I had one of them big fat to-maters right now.*
>
> *Look at him poutin. What a big baby. Don't know nuthin from nuthin. Wouldn't know enough to come in out of the rain. I guess I coulda gave him one of my taters, but then neither one of us would have the strength to keep on runnin.*
> "Can I have the skins? Please, Clint."
> "Them tater skins? Well, I threw em down in the dirt, didn't I? If I was gonna eat em, would I of throwd em down in the dirt?"

Here, we *could* use our third-person narrator to tell the readers that Billy wolfed down the potato skins, but by now, they should be used to "seeing" the story through the perceptions of the protagonist.

> *Damn, he eats like a hungry hog. Stuffed both of them tater skins into his mouth, dirt and all.*
> "Thanks, Clint. That was good."
> "It was only burnt tater skins, but you might as well have et em. If you didn't, the ants woulda."
> "They were good, Clint. I was real hungry."

We've used this nighttime middle-of-the-swamp scene to more fully establish the relationship between our two principle characters.

Now, to move the story along, let's inform the reader of the time of day. This time, we can do it using dialogue.

> "Well, you're gonna be a damn sight hungrier by tonight if you don't go back to the farm. See that yellow crack in the sky out there? It means the sun's gonna come up real soon now, and then they'll be after me again. I'm gettin back in the water, and I'm gonna keep goin til I make it to the other side of this damn swamp. If you wanna get back to the farm in time for breakfast, you'd best just wait here for em to pick ya up."
> "No, I'm gonna go with you, Clint."

By now, the reader should know Billy is not going to turn back, no matter what Clint says.

Let's continue to use protagonist thought to show Clint's two-step reaction.

> *Ignore the dummy. Just ease back into the water, and don't think about how cold it is. Now that the sun is comin, it'll warm up soon.*
> *Just keep moving. Gotta keep moving, no matter what. The other side of this swamp can't be all that far away. I'll make it. I have to make it.*

Let's continue the "rhythm" of alternating dialogue with protagonist thought.

> **"I don't feel so good, Clint."**
> **"Probably from eatin them burnt tater skins. Don't forget, it wasn't me who said to eat em."**
> **"I was hungry."**
> **"Yeah, well, if you don't go back, you're gonna get a lot hungrier."**
> **"I'm not hungry anymore."**
> **"The hell you ain't. All you had was a couple of burnt up old tater skins."**
> **"Maybe I am sort of hungry. You sure you don't got any more of them tater skins?"**
> *Ha! What a joke. If I had any more food, what makes him think I'd share it with him? Just keep movin and ignore him. If he can't keep up, well, that's his lookout.*

I'm continuing to make the Billy character gentle and accepting, while Clint remains unsympathetic.

TIP:

It is often said the reader must "**like**" the main character in a story. That's not true. In fact, many great fictional protagonists have been decidedly **unlikable**. All that is important in fiction is that the reader gets *interested* enough in the protagonist to keep reading all the way through to the end.

It's about time to get our two characters out of the swamp so we can try to find an ending to this prison-escape story. Let's move them along using the dialogue tool.

> **"Damn, how far is it across this swamp, Billy? It feels like we been wadin through this smelly water half the day."**

> "Just a little father now, Clint. There's a blacktop road on the other side."
>
> "A blacktop road? A highway? Really?"
>
> "Didn't you know that?"
>
> "Well, maybe I did and maybe I didn't, but if there really is a highway, then that'll be my ticket out of this damn state. The last they'll see of me is my backend gettin clean away from here."
>
> "Where will you go, Clint?"
>
> "Well, I don't know for sure. Out of this state, that's for sure. Somewhere north. Maybe Detroit. I hear you can do about anything you want in Detroit."
>
> "Oh gosh, Clint, I think something bit me."
>
> "Bit ya?"
>
> "I think so. It hurts."
>
> "Probly a snake. Most likely."
>
> "If it was a water moccasin type snake, it'll kill me, Clint. One of my daddy's huntin pals died from a water moccasin."
>
> "Well, it'd be too bad if you died now, Billy, when we're almost outta this swamp and home free."

We're almost finished with the swamp scene (assuming we aren't going to let Billy die from a snake bite). Using dialogue, I've created the idea that there's a highway on the other side of the swamp. That highway might actually give them a way to escape; that is, if I don't insert a plot complication, which of course, I will. I can do it using the other "watcher" characters. I went to all the trouble of creating them back at the beginning of the story, so it must be about time to bring them back into the story.

> White-hair leans against the prison van. He's using his beat-up old hat as a fan to try to cool down his sweating face. "I told ya they'd make us go along on the chase. But we didn't catch em, did we? I told ya that Clint guy was fast. Didn't I tell ya?"
>
> "Yeah," says one-eye. "But all he did was run right smack into that swamp. We mighta's well a stopped chasin right then. They'll never come out of that

> swamp alive. No use us even waitin for em here. The crocs'll have got em by now, and that means I win the bet."
>
> "I wouldn't go countin your winnins just yet. You can't never count out a runner like that Clint. And don't forget he's got Poor Billy along with him. Poor Billy is from around here. Mark my words, there's a good chance they can make it through the swamp."
>
> "Shut up, you two," says the guard. "Just keep your eyes open. This is the only road anywhere near the swamp. If they come out, this is where they'll try to get to."

I've re-introduced the two old trustees and the guard.

I used the narrator to keep the reader in the scene (White-hair leans against the prison van) and to convey information about the environment and the time of day (his sweating face).

Now the reader will know what is waiting for our two main characters when they come out of the swamp. That creates plot. Will the reader expect, or hope, they will get caught and taken back to the prison? Or will they hope that they can somehow still find a way to get away?

> *Patches of dry land. Must be gettin close to the other side. Once I'm out of this damned swamp, I'll find that highway and hitch a ride. Or hop a train. Get back up north to a big city where a man can have some fun.*
>
> "I see a road ahead, Clint. And a car."
>
> "Yeah, I see em. It's the prison van. Damn it!"
>
> "Does it mean we're caught, Clint?"
>
> "They're waiting for us to come outta this swamp. And they got them dogs to sniff us out if we don't. Damn, damn, damn. I sure as hell don't want ta go back."
>
> "I'm not feelin so good, Clint. And I'm hungry. Maybe I wouldn't mind going back."
>
> "You sure you wanna go back, Billy? They'll tack on more time to your sentence."
>
> "I don't even know what my sentence is, Clint.

They never told me."

"Well, I'm not goin back. Even if I have to stay in
the swamp. I'd rather die in a damn swamp than go
back to that prison."

Billy grabs Clint's arm. "I could tell em you got
away, Clint. I could tell em you're already gone."

Clint pries Poor Billy's grip off of his arm. "And
how do you spose I coulda got away, Billy? What
would you tell em? That I flew away like a bird?"

Billy scratches his head while he thinks about that.
"Well, I could tell em . . . I could tell em you got in a
car and drove away. That's what I could tell em."

"You'd do that, Billy? You'd do that for me?"

"Sure I would. Cause you gave me somethin to eat
when I was hungry."

"Nuthin but a couple of burnt tater skins."

"And you let me stay in your hole with you when I
was cold. That was nice."

Billy continues his "nice guy" behavior, willing to help his
"friend" Clint, even if it means he will have to go back to prison.
Should we make his plan work?

Let's let the plan play out in dialogue.

"Well, it's up to you, Billy. I don't know if you can
convince em I'm gone, but it's worth a try. You go out
there and give yourself up. Tell em I got into a car and
took off down the road and left you behind. Now listen
to me, Billy. You tell em I made you come with me.
You tell em you didn't want to go, but I made you go
because you knew how to get through the swamp, and
I didn't. That way, they might not add any time to
your sentence."

"That don't matter, Clint. I got nowhere else to go
since my daddy died. Will you come back and visit
me?"

"Whatta ya mean, visit ya? How could I visit ya, if I
was to get away?"

"Then, would you . . . send me a letter?"

> "A letter? You mean when I get somewhere? I guess I could do that. If I remember."
>
> "All right, Clint. I'll say you got into a car and went away. Uh, what kind of car was it?"
>
> "What kind of car? Hell, I don't care. Any kind of car. Just tell em somebody was waitin for me at the road, and I got into a car and took off."
>
> "They'll ask me what kind of car. My daddy had a Ford. Should I say it was a Ford?"
>
> "Okay, okay, tell em it was a Ford. A black Ford."
>
> "Alright, Clint. I'll tell em it was a black Ford. I'll tell em you left already. I hope they don't catch you, Clint."
>
> "Why should they catch me? They'll think I got clean away in that black Ford. They won't even be lookin for me anymore."

Billy's plan brings us to the start of the denouement in which we wrap up all the loose ends and bring the story to a close.

How should we show the plan evolve? We have several choices. We *could* use the narrator to "tell" the reader what happens, but by now you know that is our last resort.

Now that our "watcher" characters are back in the story, we could show it through their perceptions. Or, we could use protagonist thought and have Clint stay hidden in the swamp, watching it all play out. Let's go with that option.

> *Jesus, he's walkin right straight at em. Will they believe him?*
>
> *Damn. They grabbed him and threw him down on the ground. They shouldn't have done that. Poor Billy would never hurt anybody. And now, that damn guard's got him hooked up in handcuffs. Looks like he's askin Billy some questions.*

Now we have (through Clint's perception) Billy up at the highway talking to our watcher characters. Let's switch to that scene to find out if Billy's plan is going to work.

"All right, says the guard, "spill it. How'd you get across that swamp without bein eaten by the crocs?"

"We waded, "says Billy. "We waded for a long time. It got dark, and I was cold. Can't I go back home now? I'm hungry."

"And where's your partner, Billy? Where's Clint?"

"There was a car. A black Ford."

"There was a car waitin for him?"

"Yes, Boss. A black Ford."

The guard shakes his finger in Billy's face. "Now listen, Billy. You got to tell me the truth. Otherwise, it'll go hard on you when we get you back to the farm. You understand?"

"I will tell you the truth, Boss. I didn't like it in that swamp. It was cold, and something bit me."

"No, I mean about Clint gettin away. You sure he got in a car, and the car drove away?"

"Yes, Boss. It was a Ford, like I said. A black Ford."

The white-haired trustee steps forward. "We'd better get after him, Boss."

The guard scratches at the back of his neck. "Well, I'm not so sure. How do we know Billy's not making this up? I didn't see any black Ford around anywhere. Maybe we'd better wait here. I can call the state police and have them be on the lookout for this so-called black Ford."

I think it's time to bring the white-haired trustee back into the story. After all, he does have a bet that Clint is going to get away.

"No, really," says Billy. "He got in a car and went away. Just before you got here. They went that way," He points toward the south.

The white-haired trustee also points toward the south. "There *was* a black Ford on the road, Boss. Didn't you see it?"

"What? You saw a black car?"

"Sure did, Boss. And it was goin that way." He

> points. "Just like Billy said."
> "Damn," says the guard. "Slipped right past us.
> Well, let's go get him."

To finish, let's create one more scene with the "watcher" characters.

> Sitting together with one-eye in the back of the
> prison van, white-hair says, "Told ya he'd get away."
> He holds out his hand. "Pay up."
> One-eye forks over his half dollar and his quarter.
> He looks back toward the swamp. "Damn. I never
> thought they'd make it through that swamp, what
> with them crocs and them snakes. Nobody else ever
> done that before."
> "Yeah," says white-hair,"but that Clint was fast.
> Didn't I tell ya he was a runner? If anybody coulda
> done it, it was bound to be him."

And now we can switch back to protagonist thought to let the reader know what Clint thinks about the whole thing.

> *By damn, Billy done it. Somehow, he convinced em.*
> *Good old Billy. A shame he has to go back. But I guess*
> *he got so hungry, he was ready to turn himself in. Poor*
> *kid must have missed them prison meals real bad. He'll*
> *be better off back there anyhow. Now to steal some*
> *clothes off a clothes line somewhere and catch a ride.*
> *I'll head out in the opposite direction as they went, and*
> *I'll be in Detroit in no time.*

I finished the story by having Clint get away, with the help of Poor Billy, and with the unexpected help of the white-haired trustee who went along with Billy's imaginary black Ford in order to win his bet.

But is that a satisfying end to the story? It could be, but what about Clint's volatile personality and his self-centeredness? We haven't provided the reader with any indication that he is likely to change; therefore, won't the reader expect that his personality is bound to get him into trouble again?

We could end the story with his escape and let the reader imagine what might happen to him next. After all, this story is about an escape from prison, and whatever happens to him next would be a new story.

Or would it? What if we give the reader a new scene, as a sort of epilogue, to show that although Clint did manage to get away from the prison farm, his unwillingness to change his self-centered approach to life might very well land him right back in prison again. That could, in a sense, bring the story right back to the same kind of beginning, with him again planning how to escape.

In order to notify the reader of a major break in the story line, we can add some lines spaces and three centered asterisks.

---

* * *

"How long you got, Clint?"
"Don't matter. I won't be around long."
"You think you can escape? From this place? Fat chance."
If they only knew how I made it out of that prison farm. They said nobody could make it across that swamp, but I did it. And I'll find a way out of this place too. Not about to spend three to five here. Three to five for breakin in to one lousy warehouse? Not fair. But it don't matter. Now that they gave me exercise yard privileges, I'll soon be long gone from here too. And then I'll send Billy that letter like I said I would. I'll get it postmarked from some far away place, maybe California. Prove to the kid that I got away clean, just like I said I would. Those two old trustees that always sat on the porch will read my letter too. Then they'll all know it's true that I got away clean.

Once again I've placed Clint in a prison setting, and again, he's trying to figure out how to escape. Now, all I have to do is create some new "watcher" characters to again put the focus on him. Let's use third-person narration, alternating with protagonist thought, to create one final scene.

> **The guards in the towers watch Clint. They've noticed that every time he's out in the exercise yard, he walks the entire length of the wall, even when it rains, even when it's snowing. He seems to be examining the wall, poking his finger into every crack and bullet hole.**
>
> *All I need is a couple of handholds, and I'll be able to get over the top. Maybe I can chip a few little holes out of the concrete when the guards ain't lookin. That's all I need.*
>
> **Back and forth he goes, pacing next to the wall, like a caged tiger.**
>
> **The guards, in their towers, keep their rifles at the ready and make bets of cigarettes and who-goes-for-coffee runs about when he'll try to climb that high wall. Right now, the odds are three packs of cigs against two weeks of coffee runs that he'll try it before springtime.**

In this epilogue-like conclusion, I bring the story full circle with the protagonist again in prison and looking for a way to escape.

What do you think of this second ending? If you were writing this story, would you end the story with his successful escape through the swamp, or would you add this epilogue-like ending to show that the protagonist has not changed?

I'm suggesting that you learn to read like a writer. From now on, try reading every story you come across the way I've encouraged you to read these example stories. Think about the decisions the writer is making. Think about the tools and techniques the writer has used. Consciously decide whether or not you would have made the same choices. By *reading like a writer*, you can begin to understand how every story is "built" and why it works (or doesn't work). It's a key part of learning to be a successful writer.

Review

Below is a reprint of the completed story. As you review the story, look for the fiction-writing techniques we explored in this chapter, including:

- Developing an opening scene which conveys the most **important elements of the locale** and is **representative of the environment** in which the majority of the story events will take place.
- Introducing the reader to the world of the story through **protagonist perception** to create **vicarious involvement** with the protagonist.
- Getting the reader **vicariously involved** with the protagonist through the use of the **two-step.**
- Using **third-person narration** minimally to set scenes and to show what characters in the story are doing.
- Using **regional dialect** to characterize and to indicate the locale.
- Relaying information about **the situation** through **protagonist thought** and through the observations of "watcher" characters.
- **Characterizing the protagonist** by showing the unique way he sees the situation.
- Using multiple **points of view** to show the action of the story, but **restricting internal (direct) thought to the protagonist.**
- Indicating the **passage of time** through the use of **dialogue** and **character thought**.
- Using third-person narration to provide the reader with information about the **supporting-cast characters**.
- Making sure each of the **supporting-cast characters**—although they may be unnamed—has a **specific role** in the story.
- Making sure **supporting-cast characters** are described in terms of their **role in the story** rather than who they might be as individual persons.
- Keeping the reader **in the scene**.
- Avoiding scene details that are **not relevant** to the ongoing story.

- Providing the reader with story-related events that occurred before the time frame of the story (**backstory**) through the use of **protagonist memory**, rather than through the use of **flashback**.

- Avoiding story **dilution** by providing only story information that is relevant to the story.

- Getting significant story events and scene details down on the paper in a way **the reader** can "see" them (i.e. avoiding the "**in the writer's head**" problem).

- Using **foreshadowing** to tip off the reader that a new story event or a new supporting-cast character may eventually play an important role in the story.

- Using **dialogue** and the **eavesdropping technique** to provide story information to the reader.

Escaper

Clint walks the fenceline. He's waiting for his chance to make a break for it.

Inside his brain, there is a terrible heat. The heat is fueled by anger and resentment. It burns, day and night. It drives him, makes demands of him.

As he paces along next to the fence, Clint can't stop thinking about how he got railroaded into this place. Plead guilty, they said, and you'll get a deal. Get a reduced sentence. Get to serve your time on the honor farm. *Some deal. Two to five. Not fair. The guy didn't even die for Christ's sake. They call this place an honor farm, but it's still a damn prison. Locked up at night. A guard up in his wooden tower, rifle in his hands. That makes it a damn prison, whatever they wanna to call it.*

Supper is over, and the two old trustees are sitting on the bunkhouse porch watching Clint prowl along the fenceline. They look at each other and nod in agreement: Clint will run, and tonight will be the night. They smoke their cigarettes and wait for it.

Poor Billy is a young man who's bigger than most of the other prisoners, but he sometimes seems to act more like a child. Billy is also watching Clint. He's sitting in the dirt behind the edge of the bunkhouse playing with his little twigs. Billy likes to twist his little pieces of twigs together to make them into stick people. His twig people are being held inside a prison with a fence that's made out of bigger twigs. He likes to pretend his twig people are real, and only he has control over them.

Billy likes Clint, even if nobody else does. He likes Clint because Clint is world-smart. Billy wishes he would have got the chance to go places and do things so he could be world-smart too. But no, he had to stay at home for his whole life and help his daddy with the hunting and fishing. He didn't even get to go to a school, not once. His daddy said, What would be the use a learnin how to read and write? Would it help you know where the crocs and the fish hide in the swamp? Would it help you track an animal through the forest?

Billy thinks Clint is his friend because Clint once gave Billy a little bit of the food he stole from the kitchen. When Clint slipped the food to him, he'd said, "You didn't see nuthin, did you Billy? This will be our little secret, right?"

Billy has kept their little secret since that day. Even when they lined everybody up and said nobody was gonna get to eat supper unless they fessed up about who took that food from the kitchen, Billy kept his mouth shut. Poor Billy is good at keeping his mouth shut. And he's good at watching too.

The guard in the tower is also watching Clint. He's seen it before: when one of the prisoners starts to pace next to the sagging barbed-wire fence, it means he's thinking about making a run for it. Even though the guard assumes a wiry-thin guy like Clint is probably pretty fast, he knows nobody is faster than a bullet, so he keeps his rifle in his hands, the safety off.

He suspects Clint will wait until it gets a bit darker, and then, just before the prisoners get called in for nighttime lockup, he'll make a run for it.

Clint knows the guard is watching him closely, but he's been watching the guard closely too. He's learned that the guard puts down his rifle whenever he lights a cigarette. He cups his hands around the match to protect it from the wind, even if there is no wind. *The next time he puts down the rifle to light his cigarette, that'll be when I go.*

Back on the porch, the senior trustee, the one with the full head of white hair (that he's quite proud of), says, "I'm tellin ya, tonight is the night. He's a gettin ready to run. And once he goes, he'll be fast."

"Yeah, well, that may be," says the one-eyed trustee, taking a big draw off of his loose-rolled cigarette, "but (here he points to the west with his cigarette-yellowed first finger) how's he think he's gonna get through the swamp? He may be fast, but that won't help him one bit once he's got hisself in that damn swamp. Man's gotta have a boat to get through that swamp. Otherwise, crocs. And snakes. Don't forget bout them crocs and them snakes."

"Yeah, there's crocs," says white-hair, "and they sure as hell is plenty snakes, but it won't matter to a runner like Clint. He don't care about crocs and snakes. He got to run, so run he will."

"I got a half of a dollar and a quarter right here in my pocket," says one-eye. "My money says he won't make it through the swamp."

"You bet I'll take that bet," says white-hair. "'He'll make it cause when he goes, it'll be quick, like a sudden wind at night, the kind of wind that wakes you up, but when you lie there lookin up in the dark, it's already done gone."

"Well, they can't make me chase after him," says one-eye. "Even my good leg is gettin bad now. And don't forget they got them trackin dogs. They don't need us."

"They'll make us go along," says white-hair. "You can count on it. And if he makes it to the swamp, they'll put us in a boat to go in there after him. Back before you got here, they made me a chaser. And let me tell ya, it was spooky out there all night in a boat. You could hear things movin in the water. Weird sounds, squawks and growls like I can't describe."

"Did you catch the guy?" asks one-eye.

"No, but we found his clothes. All bloody."

"Croc?"

"I spect."

Clint knows that when it gets just a bit darker, it'll be time for the call-in. That means he's got to make his break for it pretty soon. It's taken weeks of study, but by now he knows every inch of the fenceline. He knows there is one place where the barb-wire fence is weak, a place where it sags low enough for a man to make it over in one quick movement. Now all he has to do is wait for the guard to put down his rifle to light his cigarette. It's been almost an hour since that guard's last fag, so he'll be needin one soon.

Clint turns to look at the two old trustees that are sitting on the porch. *Those two are always watchin. But who cares about them. Two old lifers. Probably couldn't run down a three-legged dog if their life depended on it.*

There's the flare of the guard's match. Time to go.

The rifle shots bring the two trustees to their feet.

"I can't see clear," says one-eye. "Did the guard get him?"

"Don't think so," says white-hair. "No, now I see him. He's a runnin, and he's made it to the woods. Didn't I tell ya? Didn't I say he'd be fast?"

"Yeah, but you ain't got my money yet. He still got to get through that swamp."

What the two trustees didn't see in all the excitement, and what the guard who was climbing down from his guard tower didn't see, was that Poor Billy also took off. Over the fence and into the woods he went, chasing after Clint, like a dog chasing after his master.

Clint is sweating and breathing hard by the time he makes it into the woods, but his successful escape proves his plan was a good one. He heard shots, and he heard one of the bullets hit the ground behind him, but once he made it into the woods, there was no way that damn guard could get another shot off at him. He's not happy that his hands and knees got a bit cut up going over that damned barb-wire fence, but he tells himself not to worry about that; the bleeding will stop soon. The important thing is, he's free!

But no sooner does he have that thought when he realizes he'll have to keep running hard cause they'll soon be comin with their trackin dogs. He knows his only chance is to get to the swamp before the dogs come.

"Wait for me, Clint. You're running too fast."

Clint is startled by the voice coming out of the darkness behind him. He turns to see who it is.

"What the hell ya think yer doin, Billy? You can't come with me. You gotta go back. And right now!"

"But I don't want to go back, Clint. I want to go with you."

"Well, ya can't. Where I'm goin, you don't wanna be. Now git!"

But Billy does not turn back. He just stands there staring down at his worn-out old shoes.

Why did Poor Billy follow me? Musta seen me go over the fence and just followed. Like a dog followin a kid to school. What a dummy. Don't know nuthin about nothin. Born out in the country, I bet. For damn sure he's not a smart city guy like me. Probably never been anywhere out of this county til he ended up locked up in that prison farm. Probably got caught following somebody else when they went in to rob a store, or somethin like that. I'd better just ignore him and run faster. He'll never be able to keep up with me.

"I'm tired of running, Clint. Where we going?"

Clint is again startled to find that Billy is somehow keeping up with him. *Damn. How'd that big dummy even figure out which way I went? The last thing I need is him followin me.*

Clint stops and points back toward the prison farm. "Of course you're gettin tired, Billy. And I'm gonna be movin even faster from now on, so you won't be able to keep up. You'd best just go back now. So long, Billy."

Billy will hafta go back now. Don't know why he followed me in the first place. Gotta keep movin. They'll be comin soon with those damn dogs.

Clint leaves Billy standing there and goes back to running. Although a rusty gold moon has come up to hover just above the horizon, it's still very dark, so he often trips and falls. But each time, he gets up and continues on, cursing under his breath.

"Please, Clint, you're running too fast. I can't hardly keep up."

Damn. He's still there. Doesn't seem to matter how fast I run, he's always right behind. How does he run so fast in the dark? If they catch me now, they'll think I dragged him along intentional.

Clint stops and shakes his finger at Billy. "Now listen here, Billy. I'm headin for the swamp. You gotta go back now. I can't have you taggin along after me. You hear?"

"But this isn't the way to the swamp, Clint. You're going the wrong way."

"The hell you say. They told me the swamp was straight west of the prison, and that's what I been doin. Goin west."

Billy shakes his head. "I don't think this is the right way, Clint."

"Now Billy, ya tellin me you think you know the way to the swamp?"

"Sure, Clint. I was born and brought up around here. Right over . . . " He points. "That way."

Does this big dummy really think he knows his way around these woods in the dark? He's probably as lost as I am. They said the swamp was to the west, so I'll just keep runnin in that direction til I find it. Once they bring out the dogs, that swamp water'll cover my scent. And once I'm through the swamp and on the other side, I'll be home free. All I got to do is just keep on runnin.

"I been waiting here for you, Clint. I hear dogs. They're getting closer."

Oh, no. *I been runnin and runnin, and somehow Billy's got ahead of me. Have I been runnin in circles?*

"I'm afraid of those dogs, Clint. What if they catch us?"

"Pipe down, Billy. If you don't quit blabbin, they will catch us. Them dogs can hear talkin a mile off."

Billy whispers, "I'm sorry, Clint. I'll be real quiet."

"Now you got to tell me, Billy, do you really know the way to the swamp? You got to tell me true if you don't."

"It's right over yonder, Clint." He points. "Not too far."

Maybe he does know the way. I'm so lost, God help me if he don't.

"I changed my mind, Billy. You can go with me. But we got to get to that swamp fore the dogs come. How about you show me the way."

I'll let him lead me in the right direction, and then I'll git goin on my own. He won't be able to keep up with me, and then, when the dogs come, they'll go for him fore they get to me.

"Here's the swamp, Clint. I told you I knew where it was."

By God, the dummy really did know the way. Now I can lose them dogs in the water. Gotta move fast.

"I know how to find the swamp cause me and my daddy used to come here crawdaddin. We'd put a piece of gristle meat on a string and—"

"Sush, Billy. I got no time for your nonsense. You got me to the swamp, but best you go back now."

"But, Clint—"

"I said no! Didn't you hear me say no? Now git!"

"Why do we have to be in this water, Clint? I'm cold."

"Jesus, you scared me, Billy. You been followin me all this time?"

"I'm sorry, Clint."

"Of course you're sorry, cause you're cold. It's what you get for not doin what I said. You shoulda knowed it was gonna be cold in this damn swamp. You think I'm not cold too? When you're up to your ass in water hour after hour, you're gonna get cold, right? I told you to go back, but did you do it? No. So now you're cold. Too bad, but it's your own damn fault."

"But I'm really cold, Clint. I'm shakin."

"It's called shiverin, Billy. You don't think I'm shiverin too. It's natural when you get real cold. You got to be tough, like me. The sun'll come up by and by. Then, we'll be okay, long as the crocs don't get us."

"There aren't any crocs left in this swamp, Clint. My daddy said he and his friends caught em all. For the meat."

"Really? Well, thank heaven for that. It means I'm gonna make it. Ha! And they said I couldn't do it."

"But there's land in the middle of this swamp, Clint. Why don't we go there?"

"Land? Bull. There's nothin in this damned swamp but water and more water."

"I know where there's land, Clint. Can't we go there?"

"Well, if you think there's land in this godforsaken swamp, just show the way. But I'll believe it when I see it."

When Billy really does lead them to a small island of dry land in the middle of the swamp, Clint is amazed. "By God, Billy, you did find us a speck of dry land. Don't know how you find your way in the dark. Maybe you got them cat eyes."

"It's always dry here, Clint. Me and my daddy used to come here fishin."

"That may be, Billy boy, but we got no time for fishin. We'd better just sit tight here and wait for the dawn. Them dogs won't be able to track us here with all that water around us."

Wind's picking up. Wet clothes. Too cold. Better dig a trench. Get down out of the wind.

"Why you digging with that stick, Clint?"

"Why you think, you ninny? I'm trying to get out of the wind. Leave me alone."

"I can help you dig, Clint."

"I don't need your help, Billy. Dig your own."

"Can't I be in your hole with you?"

"What? Are you queer or somethin'? Get away from me."

"I just thought it'd be warmer for both of us."

"Well, I don't want you anywhere near me. I don't need you to keep me warm. I don't need you for nuthin. I been on my own since I was twelve, and I never asked nobody for nuthin. Just leave me alone."

So now he shuts up. Not a peep out of him. Just sits there starin at the ground, shiverin and poutin.

Damn, it's cold in these wet clothes. How can it be so cold? I shoulda gone further south before I got myself throwd in jail. I coulda made it all the way to Florida if I hadn't a stopped. But no, I had to hop off that damn train in some backwater town, some hell-and-gone place with nuthin to do there cept get drunk. And then, that smart ass had to go and insult me. Okay, so I hit the guy. So what? I've hit lots of guys before, and none of em went and got themselfs checked into no hospital. A club, the cops said. Said I hit him with a club. A club? It wasn't no damn club. It was only a damn pool cue. You can't call a normal old pool cue a club.

Clint lets the heat and resentment of memory lull him to sleep,

Billy stays where he is for a while, but soon grows so cold, he has to creep closer to Clint to try to find a place out of the wind.

Clint sits bolt upright and yells, "Croc!"

"No, it's only me, Clint. I got too cold."

Jesus. It's only the dummy. "Whatta think you're doin, Billy? Don't you ever touch me like that again when I'm asleep. You scared the hell out of me."

"I'm sorry, Clint, I got real cold."

"Well, I'm cold too. Damn cold. But didn't I tell you to stay away from me?"

"I'm sorry, Clint. I thought if we were in the same hole, we'd both be warmer."

"Well, maybe that's so. Just maybe. But if you're gonna be in my hole, you can't move. You got that? You don't move a muscle til the sun comes up."

"All right, Clint. Just let me get covered up, and then I won't move any more."

Now what's the ninny doing? Jesus, he's coverin himself up with dirt. Probably thinks he'll be warmer that way. What a dummy. Gettin himself all covered up in dirt.

And now he's sound asleep. How can anybody go to sleep that fast, what with the cold and the wind and them dogs barking in the distance?

But maybe covering himself up with dirt wasn't such a bad idea after all. Maybe I should try it. I'll be back in the water soon, and

the dirt will all wash off anyhow.

Damn the long night. Why does the night have to be so long? And so damn cold. Maybe I need some food in my stomach to warm me up.

Clint carefully unwraps his secret stash of food, trying not to wake Billy up.

"You got food, Clint?"

"So you're awake now are ya? Slept like a baby, didn't ya? While I had to lay awake here all night keepin watch out for them crocs and them snakes. Well, all I got is a couple a near burnt up taters nobody else wanted. You wouldn't like em. "

"But I'm hungry, Clint."

"Well, too damn bad. There's not enough for both a us."

"Please, Clint."

"You shoulda thought about gettin hungry fore you took off after me. I didn't ask you to come along, did I? Did you hear me askin you to come along? No. Now if you think I'm gonna share my food with you, you got another think comin."

So now he's gone back to poutin again. Watchin me eat with his one stupid tear makin a track through the dirt on his face, all the way down to his chin. Looks like the trail a snail leaves when it walks across a fat red to-mater. Man, I wish I had one of them big fat to-maters right now.

Look at him poutin. What a big baby. Don't know nuthin from nuthin. Wouldn't know enough to come in out of the rain. I guess I coulda gave him one of my taters, but then neither one of us would have the strength to keep on runnin.

"Can I have the skins? Please, Clint."

"Them tater skins? Well, I threw em down in the dirt, didn't I? If I was gonna eat em, would I of throwd em down in the dirt?"

Damn, he eats like a hungry hog. Stuffed both of them tater skins into his mouth, dirt and all.

"Thanks, Clint. That was good."

"It was only burnt tater skins, but you might as well have et em. If you didn't, the ants woulda."

"They were good, Clint. I was real hungry."

"Well, you're gonna be a damn sight hungrier by tonight if you don't go back to the farm. See that yellow crack in the sky out there? It means the sun's gonna come up real soon now, and then they'll be after me again. I'm gettin back in the water, and

I'm gonna keep goin til I make it to the other side of this damn swamp. If you wanna get back to the farm in time for breakfast, you'd best just wait here for em to pick ya up."

"No, I'm gonna go with you, Clint."

Ignore the dummy. Just ease back into the water, and don't think about how cold it is. Now that the sun is comin, it'll warm up soon.

Just keep moving. Gotta keep moving, no matter what. The other side of this swamp can't be all that far away. I'll make it. I have to make it.

"I don't feel so good, Clint."

"Probably from eatin them burnt tater skins. Don't forget, it wasn't me who said to eat em."

"I was hungry."

"Yeah, well, if you don't go back, you're gonna get a lot hungrier."

"I'm not hungry anymore."

"The hell you ain't. All you had was a couple of burnt up old tater skins."

"Maybe I am sort of hungry. You sure you don't got any more of them tater skins?"

Ha! What a joke. If I had any more food, what makes him think I'd share it with him? Just keep movin and ignore him. If he can't keep up, well, that's his lookout.

"Damn, how far is it across this swamp, Billy? It feels like we been wadin through this smelly water half the day."

"Just a little father now, Clint. There's a blacktop road on the other side."

"A blacktop road? A highway? Really?"

"Didn't you know that?"

"Well, maybe I did and maybe I didn't, but if there really is a highway, then that'll be my ticket out of this damn state. The last they'll see of me is my backend gettin clean away from here."

"Where will you go, Clint?"

"Well, I don't know for sure. Out of this state, that's for sure. Somewhere north. Maybe Detroit. I hear you can do about anything you want in Detroit."

"Oh gosh, Clint, I think something bit me."

"Bit ya?"

"I think so. It hurts."

"Probly a snake. Most likely."

"If it was a water moccasin type snake, it'll kill me, Clint. One of my daddy's huntin pals died from a water moccasin."

"Well, it'd be too bad if you died now, Billy, when we're almost outta this swamp and home free."

White-hair leans against the prison van. He's using his beat-up old hat as a fan to try to cool down his sweating face. "I told ya they'd make us go along on the chase. But we didn't catch em, did we? I told ya that Clint guy was fast. Didn't I tell ya?"

"Yeah," says one-eye. "But all he did was run right smack into that swamp. We mighta's well a stopped chasin right then. They'll never come out of that swamp alive. No use us even waitin for em here. The crocs'll have got em by now, and that means I win the bet."

"I wouldn't go countin your winnins just yet. You can't never count out a runner like that Clint. And don't forget he's got Poor Billy along with him. Poor Billy is from around here. Mark my words, there's a good chance they can make it through the swamp."

"Shut up, you two," says the guard. "Just keep your eyes open. This is the only road anywhere near the swamp. If they come out, this is where they'll try to get to."

Patches of dry land. Must be gettin close to the other side. Once I'm out of this damned swamp, I'll find that highway and hitch a ride. Or hop a train. Get back up north to a big city where a man can have some fun.

"I see a road ahead, Clint. And a car."

"Yeah, I see em. It's the prison van. Damn it!"

"Does it mean we're caught, Clint?"

"They're waiting for us to come outta this swamp. And they got them dogs to sniff us out if we don't. Damn, damn, damn. I sure as hell don't want ta go back."

"I'm not feelin so good, Clint. And I'm hungry. Maybe I wouldn't mind going back."

"You sure you wanna go back, Billy? They'll tack on more time to your sentence."

"I don't even know what my sentence is, Clint. They never told me."

"Well, I'm not goin back. Even if I have to stay in the swamp. I'd rather die in a damn swamp than go back to that prison."

Billy grabs Clint's arm. "I could tell em you got away, Clint. I could tell em you're already gone."

Clint pries Poor Billy's grip off of his arm. "And how do you spose I coulda got away, Billy? What would you tell em? That I flew away like a bird?"

Billy scratches his head while he thinks about that. "Well, I could tell em . . . I could tell em you got in a car and drove away. That's what I could tell em."

"You'd do that, Billy? You'd do that for me?"

"Sure I would. Cause you gave me somethin to eat when I was hungry."

"Nuthin but a couple of burnt tater skins."

"And you let me stay in your hole with you when I was cold. That was nice."

"Well, it's up to you, Billy. I don't know if you can convince em I'm gone, but it's worth a try. You go out there and give yourself up. Tell em I got into a car and took off down the road and left you behind. Now listen to me, Billy. You tell em I made you come with me. You tell em you didn't want to go, but I made you go because you knew how to get through the swamp, and I didn't. That way, they might not add any time to your sentence."

"That don't matter, Clint. I got nowhere else to go since my daddy died. Will you come back and visit me?"

"Whatta ya mean, visit ya? How could I visit ya, if I was to get away?"

"Then, would you . . . send me a letter?"

"A letter? You mean when I get somewhere? I guess I could do that. If I remember."

"All right, Clint. I'll say you got into a car and went away. Uh, what kind of car was it?"

"What kind of car? Hell, I don't care. Any kind of car. Just tell em somebody was waitin for me at the road, and I got into a car and took off."

"They'll ask me what kind of car. My daddy had a Ford. Should I say it was a Ford?"

"Okay, okay, tell em it was a Ford. A black Ford."

"Alright, Clint. I'll tell em it was a black Ford. I'll tell em you left already. I hope they don't catch you, Clint."

"Why should they catch me? They'll think I got clean away in that black Ford. They won't even be lookin for me anymore."

Jesus, he's walkin right straight at em. Will they believe him?

Damn. They grabbed him and threw him down on the ground. They shouldn't have done that. Poor Billy would never hurt anybody. And now, that damn guard's got him hooked up in handcuffs. Looks like he's askin Billy some questions.

"All right, says the guard, "spill it. How'd you get across that swamp without bein eaten by the crocs?"

"We waded, "says Billy. "We waded for a long time. It got dark, and I was cold. Can't I go back home now? I'm hungry."

"And where's your partner, Billy? Where's Clint?"

"There was a car. A black Ford."

"There was a car waitin for him?"

"Yes, Boss. A black Ford."

The guard shakes his finger in Billy's face. "Now listen, Billy. You got to tell me the truth. Otherwise, it'll go hard on you when we get you back to the farm. You understand?"

"I will tell you the truth, Boss. I didn't like it in that swamp. It was cold, and something bit me."

"No, I mean about Clint gettin away. You sure he got in a car, and the car drove away?"

"Yes, Boss. It was a Ford, like I said. A black Ford."

The white-haired trustee steps forward. "We'd better get after him, Boss."

The guard scratches at the back of his neck. "Well, I'm not so sure. How do we know Billy's not making this up? I didn't see any black Ford around anywhere. Maybe we'd better wait here. I can call the state police and have them be on the lookout for this so-called black Ford."

"No, really," says Billy. "He got in a car and went away. Just before you got here. They went that way," He points toward the south.

The white-haired trustee also points toward the south. "There *was* a black Ford on the road, Boss. Didn't you see it?"

"What? You saw a black car?"

"Sure did, Boss. And it was goin that way." He points." Just like Billy said."

"Damn," says the guard. "Slipped right past us. Well, let's go get him."

Sitting together with one-eye in the back of the prison van, white-hair says, "Told ya he'd get away." He holds out his hand. "Pay up."

One-eye forks over his half dollar and his quarter. He looks back toward the swamp. "Damn. I never thought they'd make it through that swamp, what with them crocs and them snakes. Nobody else ever done that before."

"Yeah," says white-hair, "but that Clint was fast. Didn't I tell ya he was a runner? If anybody coulda done it, it was bound to be him."

By damn, Billy done it. Somehow, he convinced em. Good old Billy. A shame he has to go back. But I guess he got so hungry, he was ready to turn himself in. Poor kid must have missed them prison meals real bad. He'll be better off back there anyhow. Now to steal some clothes off a clothes line somewhere and catch a ride. I'll head out in the opposite direction as they went, and I'll be in Detroit in no time.

* * *

"How long you got, Clint?"

"Don't matter. I won't be around long."

"You think you can escape? From this place? Fat chance."

If they only knew how I made it out of that prison farm. They said nobody could make it across that swamp, but I did it. And I'll find a way out of this place too. Not about to spend three to five here. Three to five for breakin in to one lousy warehouse? Not fair. But it don't matter. Now that they gave me exercise yard privileges, I'll soon be long gone from here too. And then I'll send Billy that letter like I said I would. I'll get it postmarked from some far away place, maybe California. Prove to the kid that I got away clean, just like I said I would. Those two old trustees that always sat on the porch will read my letter too. Then they'll all know that I got away clean.

The guards in the towers watch Clint. They've noticed that every time he's out in the exercise yard, he walks the entire length of the wall, even when it rains, even when it's snowing. He seems to be examining the wall, poking his finger into every crack and bullet hole.

All I need is a couple of handholds, and I'll be able to get over the top. Maybe I can chip a few little holes out of the concrete when the guards ain't lookin. That's all I need.

Back and forth he goes, pacing next to the wall, like a caged tiger.

The guards, in their towers, keep their rifles at the ready and make bets of cigarettes and who-goes-for-coffee runs about when he'll try to climb that high wall. Right now, the odds are three packs of cigs against two weeks of coffee runs that he'll try it before springtime.

5

Rewriting and Revision

Revision is a key aspect of the fiction-writing *process*. No matter what type of story you are writing, you can't complete it without the revision stage.

The name of this chapter is "Rewriting and Revision," but is rewriting different than revision? Not really, but you don't want to think of *revision* as just "fixing." The term *"rewriting"* reminds you that during the revision process you will undoubtedly have to entirely rewrite some things.

Whether you call it revision or rewriting, it is important to remember that the process involves *rethinking*. That means that some parts of your "finished" story may have to be rewritten, moved, or entirely removed.

Because revision is such a crucial aspect of writing a story, you shouldn't worry too much about the first draft. It is very freeing to *assume* that the words you are writing in the first draft of a story are not very likely be in the final draft. The first draft is just to "get to know" your character and to begin *the process* of figuring out the series of story events that will eventually lead to some kind of satisfactory conclusion by the end. You can't really *know* the character or how the situation is going to be resolved until you finish the first draft, so why waste a lot of time "perfecting" it? Instead, focus on developing an interesting character and an interesting situation, and then start the writing process by "walking" the character (putting the protagonist into the situation). As you get to know the protagonist better, the story will *evolve* as the character does what he or she "needs" to do.

Then, during the revision process, you can start to think about the final product. At this point, you can bring your focus to overall structure.

Another revision issue is looking at what I call the logic of "the chain of events." You have to learn to look at each scene you've created in terms of its purpose. All great stories are "built" as a *chain* of interlocking story events that lead the reader forward. Each scene in your story should be seen as setting up the next scene. There is no purpose to a scene in a fictional story if it does not set up a situation that requires another following scene to deal with that situation. Each link in the chain of scenes logically "connects to" (leads to) the next scene. Are there missing links in the chain? Are there unnecessary links in the chain? If one scene accomplished a task, why would you need another scene to accomplish that task again?

Another revision draft should look only at what each scene is *contributing* to the whole story. Each scene should be in the story for a reason. Each scene should accomplish a specific task.

During revision, it's important that you don't "get caught up" in reading the story. A way to do that is to do separate drafts that look for specific types of problems. Going through your entire story by *just reading it* puts you in the role of a reader, not a reviser. You will miss glaring errors that relate to overall design and execution. You should plan on doing one complete go-through that focuses only on the *overall structure*. You will also need another complete go-through that looks only at individual *scenes*, thinking, in each case, of how the reader will "see" that scene. I call that *the enriching draft*. The idea is to revisit each and every scene to see if there aren't ways to make the scene richer, more visual, and more vicariously involving. Other revision go-throughs focus on things like character motivation, sense of time passing, and realism of dialogue.

Students often ask me how many drafts are necessary. The only possible answer is, *as many as it takes*. A short story might take a half dozen drafts, but if it's not working out, it could take a lot more drafts than that.

And what about revising a novel? How many drafts should that take? Well, that's not so easy to answer either. When I'm writing a novel, *and* when I'm revising a novel, I try to spend eight hours a day at it, as if it was a normal job (a job I enjoy).

Unfortunately, not everybody can be a full-time writer. But you still have to put in however much time it takes to complete the story-writing process, and a lot of that time is going to be spent on rewriting.

As a story evolves, you will realize there are things happening that require you to go back and put in some kind of reader preparation— things like foreshadowing, plot hints, and character development. That is especially true of a novel. When that happens, I do one of two things: either I go back and insert a scene right then, or else I immediately stop and write myself a note about what needs to be done. Every writer has his or her own approach to writing, but every writer needs to develop revision and rewriting skills that get the job done.

Most importantly, in order to do *real* revision, you have to somehow get out of your writer's head and into your imagined reader's head. You have to look at every aspect of your story, trying to imagine what the reader will think. Will your readers clearly "see" each scene? Will they understand why the characters do what they do? Ask those and a hundred other reader-oriented questions, and you will end up with a great story, one that will get your readers interested and keep them engaged until they turn the last page.

Finally, you have to do what I call *the ruthless draft*; that is, a special draft in which you ask yourself questions like, "Does this really need to be in the story?" or "Did I approach this scene in entirely the wrong way?" or "Maybe this doesn't belong here." Making major changes during revision is not something most writers want to do, and that fact can prevent you from looking at your work objectively. That's why I call this final stage of revision "ruthless." You have to go into it actively *looking for* things that might be wrong, and then, you have to be willing to make the required changes, no matter how much time it takes.

In my first draft, I like to "overwrite." That is, when I'm still in the process of working out the story, I like to put in *everything* I can think of. That means the later revision process will often involve deciding what to cut out. During the ruthless draft, I *always* end up removing some of the text, sometimes quite large amounts of text. While writing your first draft, you have to *know* you will get a chance to pare it down later during the revision process.

You'd be surprised how much you can cut out of a story without changing it. When I was a graduate student, I wrote for magazines and newspapers to make tuition money. Often, the editors of such periodicals would tell me I had to remove a certain number of lines in order to make the story "fit" in the slot assigned to it. My task then became to remove the required number of lines without changing the story. I was able to do it every time, and that taught me every story can be leaned out during the revision process.

As I said earlier, one of the writer's biggest problem is the "in the writer's head" problem. During the revision process, you have to somehow get out of your head (the way you see the scene) and into your imagined reader's head. For that, you may need the kind of feedback you get from other writers in a *writing workshop*.

If all that makes the revision process sound like a lot of work, well, it is. To be a successful fiction writer, you are going to have to learn to love the process of writing *and* the process of revision. Many beginning writers enjoy the story-development process, but get impatient during the revision process. In my job as the executive director of the FictionWeek Literary Review, I read a lot of stories that *could have been* very good, if only the writer had taken time to do a little more revision. Mores the pity.

Final Thoughts

Finally, if you want to become a good fiction writer, you should try to *live the life* of a writer. That doesn't mean you have to quit your day job and try to make your living writing full time, but it does mean you have to take your "job" as a writer seriously. You can't just hang out in coffee shops with your laptop and tell your friends you really are a "real" writer. You have to create a quiet place in your home where you can work without distractions, and you have to create specific times during the day (or maybe during the weekends) to really focus on your fiction writing.

It's also a good idea to hang out with other writers. As I said earlier, because getting feedback is such an important part of the writing process, you should take a workshop-oriented university writing class or join a writing workshop at your local library. If you do that, you will not only get good feedback, you will also meet other writers. Many friendships evolve out of writing workshops because you all have something common—you are all serious writers!

You should also go to writing conferences. You may or may not learn all that much about writing at a conference, but it keeps you "in the game," and you might meet other local writers there. Local writing conferences are often sponsored by writing clubs. If so, join that club.

You should also read books about fiction writing. Don't waste your time reading books that say all you have to do is light a candle and get "inspired." Instead, look for books that describe specific fiction writing techniques.

You should also read everything you can find on the internet about writing (there is a lot, and much of it will have to be taken with a grain of salt).

What I'm saying is that, at some point, you are going to have to decide how serious you are about undertaking what is actually a very challenging endeavor.

That said, you have to be patient with yourself. As much as we all would like to buy into the fantasy of whipping out a great story and becoming famous overnight, it just doesn't work that way. Becoming a better writer takes time and practice and study. And then more prac-tice and more study.

Have you heard that fiction writing is painful? It shouldn't be, not if you see yourself as a learner. Learning to write fiction should be a satisfying and enjoyable experience.

You should think of every new writing project as an opportunity for yet another interesting learning experience. Have fun with the learning process. Try different styles of writing. Try writing things you don't know how to write. Try writing in new ways you don't think will work. Try some experimental and/or postmodern writing, just to see how many different ways there are of telling a fictional story.

If you think of yourself as *a learner*, every new writing project becomes another chance to grow and develop into the writer you want to be. Now, go do it!

About the Author

Dr. Murdock is an emeritus professor at California State University, Long Beach. He is a recipient of that university's Distinguished Faculty Teaching Award (the university's teacher of the year award). He is the Executive Editor of the FictionWeek Literary Review.

www.ingramcontent.com/pod-product-compliance
Lightning Source LLC
Chambersburg PA
CBHW071242130626
46556CB00003B/1129